The MAN *in the* WOODS

STEVE GRIFFIN

by Steve Griffin

The Ghosts of Alice:

The Boy in the Burgundy Hood
The Girl in the Ivory Dress
Alice and the Devil

The Secret of the Tirthas (young adult):

The City of Light
The Book of Life
The Dreamer Falls
The Lady in the Moon Moth Mask
The Unknown Realms

1.

I met him first in the woods.

Not the edge woods, where young couples ambled and old people walked their dogs, but the deep woods, where no one ever came. The woods you had to cycle on old dirt paths to get to, that were full of quiet and stillness, where even sunlight struggled to reach in places. My woods. Only twenty-five miles south of London, but buried so deep in the Surrey Hills you'd never know it.

It was a Saturday, the day of my accident, the day Sally got hurt so badly – the day it all kicked off. When I got up it was raining so I spent the morning fixing my ogre centurion and painting a unit of dark elves for the upcoming battle with Johnny, then helped Richard shift his old record player and LPs into the loft. He'd wanted to keep them downstairs in the alcove in the dining room, he loved his vinyl, but Joanne had insisted on a spring clean with the new baby and all. Space needed to be made, clutter cleared, and he mostly just listened to playlists on the smart speakers these days. So they had to go.

After lunch the weather was better – still cold, still cloudy, but no rain – so I took my bike out to the jumps I'd dug the weekend before. Our house is at the end of the road, right up against the woods. I cycled past our old Ford parked at an angle on the verge, rattled down the dust track, then veered sharp left up the muddy path through the trees. I followed the path for a half a mile or so, all the time on an upwards incline, then doglegged off down a narrow bike trail.

This was where it began to get good.

Moments later I was racing down the side of a hill, through a gloomy stand of pines, and the air was fierce cold against my head but I was fine and warm inside my jacket and loving it. The sandy path had collapsed at one point and I left the ground before coming down on a tricky mix of small stones and tree roots, standing on the pedals and lifting the handlebars to keep control. It was good, everything was quick and fine. I pedalled hard, breathing in the strong, damp pine scent.

After that was another long, slow uphill stretch, through some clearer, leafless trees with thick, moss-covered trunks, and then on to a level patch with occasional views across a valley to more woodland, punctuated by two empty fields. At the end of this was a clump of holly and a mishmash of thin tree stems growing from the same trunks, coppicing I think they called it. It was an area where you could never see very far ahead and had to pedal slowly to find a way through. This was my place, my kingdom, the deep wood where others didn't come.

And this was where he was.

I heard him first, hacking away at the thin, multi-stemmed trees with a billhook. Thwack, thwack, thwack, and stop. I braked sharply, halted, and peered through the dark lines of the trees. Like looking through bars, trying to see... what? A prisoner?

I spotted him, crouching down, facing away from me. My heart began to race and I felt sick.

What was he doing? Thwack, crack, thwack, his arm went up and down with that mean-looking hook. Stems fell. His other arm grabbed the wounded limbs that clung on and twisted them off. The King talked to his plants, didn't he? I could imagine them screaming.

I lay my bike down quietly in the mush of leaves and mud and crept forward, settling each foot as quietly as possible, breathing shallowly, peering. He was dressed in a padded, khaki-coloured coat, and his hair was long, possibly dreaded. From the back, he looked like a hippie. But he shouldn't be here, not this far out in the woods.

I had a flurry of feelings, predominately anxious, but there was also some anticipation, some sense of something big, auspicious even.

I watched him continuing to hack and fell, stacking his whips carefully beside him. And then he stopped, and looked up and ahead.

Even though he was facing away from me, I had the sense that he was aware of my presence. I felt an amazing, overriding sense of terror. Without thinking, I yanked up the handlebars of my bike and pedalled off as fast as I could.

I had to get away.

2.

I cycled back fast and as I saw the light through the trees and the front edge of our house I realised everything was coming to a head and instinctively I slewed through wet mud and went flying over the handlebars.

I brought my arms up and they took the brunt of my weight as I hit a tree. Still I felt my head knock the trunk and my neck jar. Next thing I was staring up through the leafless canopy at a sorry grey sky.

I groaned and lifted my forearms. The left one was streaked with a mixture of moss, mud, and a little blood. The right was just dirty.

I touched my head and looked at my fingers. There was a small amount of blood there, too.

I climbed slowly to my feet and checked the bike. As I came off I'd pushed it towards the bank of earth on the other side of the path, so luckily it wasn't damaged. There were some twigs and leaf mulch snagged in the gears. I picked them out, brushed myself down, and walked it the last few metres to the house.

As I've said, our house was on a road at the edge of Abingale, a pretty-but-dull market town full of London commuters. The street was set on a low hill, with houses on the top side only and allotments running down the other to the brook below. It had all kinds of buildings, from three-storey flats at the far (town) end to some big, rich houses in the middle, and finally some smaller, older houses at the end. Ours was the last, a small redbrick house facing the woods with a garden to the front and side and a row of cutesy cottages behind. As I said, a mishmash.

I put my bike in the shed and went in through the kitchen door. Joanne was sitting at the table drinking coffee, the baby nestled in her lap.

'Daniel! What happened?' she asked.

'Fell off my bike,' I said.

'Oh,' she said, standing up. Sally's head lolled backwards against Joanne's shoulder but her eyes remained shut. I sometimes wondered if they were ever going to open, or whether she'd sleep the rest of her life.

Joanne set the baby down in her Moses basket and fussed about my injuries. She took me over to the sink and washed my arm and then dabbed my head with some of the cotton wool she used for the baby.

'This is going to leave some nasty bruises,' she muttered. 'You need to be more careful when you're out there on your own. Supposing you fell off and broke your leg and didn't have reception? You'd be in trouble.'

I nodded but didn't say anything. All I was thinking about was the man. He was so weird, chopping down trees out there on his own. Maybe he was one of those conservationists? I thought about telling Joanne, but then realised there was no point. All her thoughts and worrying were reserved for the baby. A strange man in the woods would make her worry more.

After Joanne had finished peeling a plaster on to my forehead, Sally woke and began to wail. She still didn't open her eyes, though. I left quickly when I saw them gearing up for a breast feed. I went upstairs.

On the landing I saw the ladder was still down and the loft hatch open.

'You up there, Richard?' I called.

'Yes, nearly finished.' Richard's thin face popped out from the corner of the hatch, his long hair hanging down around it. 'Pass up that case, will you?' he said.

I lifted the suitcase and climbed the first few steps of the ladder with it, then shoved it up along the rails above my head.

'What did you do?' he asked, as he grappled it up and away.

'Fell off my bike.'

'Must be good riding, with all that fresh mud. I'll come with you tomorrow,' he said, grinning. I smiled, but knew he wouldn't. Last summer he'd spent a fortune on a top of the range mountain bike, but he'd only used it half a dozen times.

I went into my room and stepped between the carefully marshalled plastic figures I was painting up as the legions of hell. Back at my desk I checked my phone to see if Johnny had texted, but he hadn't. Then I tested the ogre centurion's spear and found it had fixed well. No permanent damage.

Outside I heard rain smattering on the leaves and the flagstones in the garden. I stared out of the window at the dark woods and thought about the man.

Could he be who I thought he was?

3

That night there was a storm and the baby cried and cried. The landing light was constantly going on and it felt like my parents were pacing all night, traipsing in and out of the cot room.

When I got up my head felt like it was packed with cotton wool from lack of sleep. I came downstairs bleary-eyed and found Richard and Joanne standing over Sally in the Moses basket. They must have put her in it early and carried her down. She was asleep now but they looked worried.

'It looks swollen to me…' Joanne was saying.

'Is she all right?' I asked.

Richard sighed and looked round at me. His skin sagged grey below his eyes.

'We think your sister has hurt her leg,' he said.

I peered into the basket and saw her left leg was pinkish-red, unlike the right one which was just pink.

'How did that happen?' I asked.

'We don't know,' said Joanne.

'She might have caught it in one of the side slats while she was asleep,' said Richard.

'We have to take her to the East Surrey,' said Joanne. She spoke quickly with nerves. Her long brown hair hung lank round her pale face.

'Yes,' said Richard.

'Aren't you going to church?' I said.

'Not today,' said Joanne. 'Richard, get the keys, we'll go straight away.'

As Richard walked out the room, Joanne said to me: 'You can stay here if you like, love. I don't know how long we'll be.'

'Sure.'

I could tell they were really worried. The baby was only eight weeks old, after all. And it had taken them so long to have their first child. Their first *natural* child.

After they'd gone I got some cereal and turned on the TV in the kitchen. The first thing that came on was a news programme, showing the Prime Minister somewhere outside, embattled amongst a group of journalists as his bodyguards tried to get him back to his black car.

'… think we should have learned from the previous botched invasions, Prime Minister?' shouted one of the reporters.

The PM obviously didn't need to stop – his guards had nearly got him into the car – but he did. As lights flashed in his face he turned to the camera and said, in his earnest, statesmanlike way:

'Look, I've explained this very carefully before. Previous administrations may have tailored their facts and evidence, but this time we have it clearly from the

UN. They now have proven nuclear capability and have stated on record that they would like to see Israel – and her allies – annihilated. We have no choice…'

'Would you call us an ally of Israel, Prime Minister? And the sheer scale of the public protest…'

I didn't have much of a head for listening to politicians and journalists, but as I watched those urgent-looking, affronted faces my head swam with ideas about the looming war. Whilst Richard and Joanne were very firmly in the anti-war camp, I wasn't so sure. If *A...* – whatever his name was – had developed nuclear weapons then surely it was a good idea to stop him? He gave the impression of being a madman, very unstable, and he made scathing verbal attacks on the West. I felt sure he was planning some major strike on us, something much worse than 9/11 or 7/7. Ignoring him felt naïve to me. Didn't you have to fight sometimes, to keep yourself and your friends safe?

And all this led straight back to the man in the woods. Was it *him*?

There was only one way to find out.

4.

I took a different route this time.

I cycled down a long, straight dirt-track, dug down into the soil with high mud banks on either side topped by tall black trees with exposed, twisted roots. Before the track finished at a small footbridge across the brook, I veered off and headed down a bed of soft pine needles in between straight, brown trunks. But before I knew it, I'd gone clean through a fresh pile of dog mess. I had to stop to clear it off my tyres with a stick. It stank and I was furious. The footbridge came in from the scrap yard, near where Mr Jackson lived. I knew it was one from his old Labrador, Toby, because that dog was dying and its business was more like a cowpat. Mr Jackson never cleared up after his dog. I liked to keep my bike clean, washed it every week, and dog mess was disgusting to get off. It filled the treads, and there was no way of properly getting it out. You had to ride through other, cleaner stuff, like sand or dusty gravel, but you always knew some of it was still there, just covered up. It didn't take much to clean it up, most dog owners did now. But Mr Jackson was old, old in a bad way, so he didn't care what happened to other people anymore. I cursed him, and cycled on and away from the fringes of the town, deeper into the forest.

After pedalling for a few minutes, the quiet began to feel strangely creepy, almost menacing. I jumped when the first thing – a crow, cawing out of sight – made a noise. The woods didn't feel right today, and I had to admit, I was nervous. I wondered if he'd still be there.

He was.

When I caught my first glimpse of him he was kneeling again, intent upon something on the ground. His thick hair hung forward as his arms and shoulders shook. Screwing up my courage, I continued to cycle slowly through the sparse copse towards him.

It didn't take long before my tyre cracked a twig. He looked up and I froze.

'Who's there?' he called.

'Me,' I said. I continued to weave through the trees towards him, knowing I'd have to get a better look at him to be sure. He didn't seem worried, and bent back down to carry on with what he was doing. As I drew near I saw he was unwinding ivy from around a small broken trunk.

I stopped a few metres away from him.

'What are you doing?' I asked.

'Getting some ivy. For cordage.' His voice was quiet, and he had a bit of an accent. It sounded like Welsh, but it might have been Scottish or something. I'm rubbish on accents. He looked up at me as he wrapped the ivy round his hand and slipped it into his big coat pocket.

'I'm not going to nick it,' I said. I realised it was a stupid thing to say, who would want to nick ivy? But something about the way he'd stuffed it away made him look apprehensive of me, so I wanted to make light of the situation. But my words died in the silence of the woods.

'Where do you live?' I asked.

As he rose to his feet I heard his joints cracking. He was a young man, but obviously he had problems. He was taller than I'd thought he would be.

'In the city,' he said.

'You were here yesterday, weren't you?'

'Yes.'

'Cutting wood.'

'Yes.'

'Are you one of those conversationists?'

He laughed.

'You mean conservationists.'

'That's what I said.'

'No, you said conversationist. Or maybe that is what you meant,' he added as I blushed. 'I suppose I'm a bit of both.'

'You're taking the mickey.'

'No.'

I wondered if he meant it, if he was telling the truth. Guessed he probably was.

His skin was pale, and he had a chestnut beard that was very patchy considering the weight of his lank, messy hair. He looked kind of ill, undernourished, but his eyes were lightning-bolt-blue, and I couldn't look at them.

'Why were you cutting trees down?'

'For the same reason I'm getting the ivy - to make a shelter.'

'Why?'

'You ask a lot of questions.'

I hated that. It wasn't going to stop me.

'You're staying out here, aren't you? You're living out here, alone in the woods.'

'Yes.'

'Wow!' I shook my head energetically. 'Like that bloke on the telly, the Bear! You're nuts…'

'I just plan to see how it goes. For a while,' he said casually, although for the first time he glanced at me askance, uncertain.

'Wow!' I repeated. 'How are you going to live? What are you going to eat?' I looked at his pockets, saw a few ivy leaves poking out. 'Are you for real?'

'I'm going to see if I can do it. People do harder things.'

'How long for?' I asked.

'A few weeks.'

'Weeks…' I mulled that for a moment. It had started to drizzle. He just stood there, his legs slightly apart. He had thick, padded boots on, the laces wrapped up around his trousers.

Then I said:

'Are you on the run?'

'No.'

'Done something wrong?' Perhaps he was a criminal, or a child abuser or something. I had to check.

'No.'

'Who are you?' I wanted to look up at his eyes but knew to keep my head down.

'You know who I am.'

5.

He *had* been on the telly, but he wasn't the bush craft guy.

He was the one who led all those protests against the Prime Minister and the war, the one who'd been camped out in front of Parliament with the others before they were evicted by the police. From the shapeless, padded jacket and the lanky hair you'd know him anywhere.

Every time the journalists wanted a sound bite they'd go to him. He had a clever way of putting things, he sounded good and everyone remembered him. He was a man campaigning for peace, but he always gave the impression of being a bit dangerous because he was so angry. Richard and Joanne were right behind him. The only people who didn't like him were the government.

For a while he was everywhere, but then a week or so ago, after another run in with the police, he disappeared. Joanne and I laughed at Richard when he said he'd been captured and locked up secretly by MI5.

Now I'd found him, living wild and alone in my woods.

And now I knew exactly who he was.

Exactly.

6.

My head was reeling as I came back home through the increasing darkness and saw the car parked up on the verge. I was wondering whether I should tell Richard and Joanne, but as soon as I got in I sensed a change in the atmosphere. In the neon light of the kitchen, Joanne was holding the baby tight in a yellow blanket, and Richard had his arms around them both. They turned and looked at me when I came in.

'Daniel – where have you been?' asked Richard.

'In the woods.'

'You could have let us know!' said Joanne. 'Sent a text.' She looked angry. Angry and worried.

I didn't say anything. I was always off cycling in the woods. I never sent texts.

'Look, son – sorry,' said Richard, breaking away from Joanne and the baby. As he did so the blanket dangled loose at the bottom, and I noticed a white bandage on Sally's leg. Richard saw me looking at it.

'Her leg's broken,' he said.

'How?'

'We don't know. We think it probably got caught in the slats of the cot.'

'Poor Sally!' I stepped up to the baby and cupped her dark hair in my hand. I kissed her on the forehead. Her eyes didn't open.

When I stepped back I could see tears growing at the corner of Joanne's eyes.

'My baby!' she said and pressed her face into Sally's.

I made them both a cup of tea and then, realising there was nothing I could do, I headed up to my room. As I sat there on my laptop, surfing war gaming blogs, I heard the rain swishing against my window, and the anguished murmur of my parents' voices downstairs.

7.

I don't like school, no one likes school, but after the freakiness of the weekend it felt reassuring to be back there next morning. Everyone in their navy uniforms, drifting from one lesson to the next, and (mostly) not having to think.

I got to the first class, Religious Studies, early, and sat halfway down. I watched as the other kids came in, telling those who tried to sit next to me that the seat was taken. I was waiting for Johnny, he hadn't replied to any of my texts and I wanted to check he was still coming at the weekend for our battle. I'd bought a whole new load of figures and already painted half of them. It was going to be the biggest fight we'd ever had.

Finally he arrived on his own, with his red backpack and his too-long white cuffs sticking out the bottom of his blazer sleeves.

'Johnny – here!' I shouted across the room, my voice too shrill. Other kids stared.

He looked over at me, and I noticed the thin black scab on his forehead covered by a couple of butterfly stitches. The corners of his lips turned up in one of his morose half-smiles and he began heading towards me, glancing around. But next moment the teacher, Miss

Hailey, arrived and then he was sitting by a girl, by Gemma Tees.

I looked down at my desk.

'So, we were talking about rituals…'

I was normally quite attentive in class but I drifted that morning, there was too much on my mind.

'… are you, Mr Page?'

I realised I'd been caught out. I looked up at Miss Hailey's youthful smirk, her soft brown eyes.

'Er – sorry Miss?'

'I asked whether you were with us or not this morning, Mr Page?' she said. The class was quiet.

'Sorry, Miss, I drifted off there. Poor night's sleep.'

'Well, I'm sorry to hear that,' she said. Johnny threw a glance back at me from under his thick, curly fringe.

'I was asking if you could tell us what the Muslims do at Ramadan?'

'They fast, Miss. But only from sunrise to sunset. They get up early to eat before dawn. It's worse for them when it comes in summer. Longer between meals.'

'Good. And why do they fast?'

'I think – there's lots of reasons. But the main one is to be closer to Allah.'

I could see she was happy, her eyes were swimming. I knew she liked me, I was good at this cultural stuff. Maths and science were a different matter.

'Thank you, Daniel. And please, get an early night tonight.'

When the lesson finished I hurried over to Johnny. He was still sitting, talking to Gemma about one of the contestants on the weekend talent show. He was making her laugh.

'I got the dark elves,' I said.

He stopped talking and looked at me.

'You coming over Saturday?'

'Might have to visit the relatives,' he said.

I looked at Gemma who was staring up at me too, her eyes bright and shiny like Miss Harvey's.

I turned and walked out of the room.

8.

I cycled home that afternoon inwardly cursing girls.

Why did they always have to come between you and your mates? I could see Gemma was cute, lots of boys in our year liked her long, dark hair, but… I didn't believe that relatives thing, couldn't he see her as well as play a war game with me? It's hardly like the two things were incompatible. There was plenty of time for both, wasn't there?

I was feeling so sore, I scarcely noticed the silver Renault pulled up on the grass verge opposite our house. It was only as I climbed off by the garden gate that I properly took it in. It was clean inside, black seats, with a folder on the dashboard. Had someone come to see us?

I pushed my bike up through the paved lower garden and put it in the shed, beneath the stone wall that retained our high lawn. As I was closing the shed door, the back door opened and a man and woman came out.

The man had curly grey hair and wore a brown fleecy jacket. He had glasses and unshaven whiskers on the tops of his cheeks. The woman was tall and stocky, with silver hair and a plump face. Her lips were full and pink.

'… next week,' I heard the man say to Joanne, who was standing behind him in the shadow of the kitchen. Joanne mumbled something in reply.

'Goodbye, Mrs Page,' said the woman, and they both turned and started walking towards me. Joanne obviously hadn't seen me, because the kitchen door slammed.

The next moment the man and woman were standing in front of me.

'Hello!' said the man. He smiled. His silver-rimmed glasses made him look kind.

'Hi,' I said.

'You must be – Daniel, is it?' said the woman. She also smiled, but it felt fake, all in the mouth, none in the eyes.

'Yeah,' I said. There was silence as I tried to work out why neither of them was quite looking into my eyes. Then I realised they were looking at the plaster on my forehead. I reached up and touched it.

'Looks like you've had a nasty bump,' said the man.

'How did you get that?' asked the woman, frowning and looking concerned.

'Who are you?'

They glanced at each other, as if checking who should reply. Somehow, it was the man.

'We're from the council,' he said. 'The social care department. I'm Paul and this is our new trainee, May, who's shadowing me. We came to see your mother. We'd heard that your baby sister wasn't well and wanted to talk to her about it.'

I frowned but didn't say anything.

'Um – is everything OK with you, Daniel?' said the woman.

'Like what?' I said.

'Like, is everything OK in the home?' asked the man.

His eyes were green, unflinching green, staring right into mine now.

9.

When I let myself in, the kitchen was full of smoke. It was Joanne who had the cigarette.

'What did they say to you?'

'Nothing,' I said, sensing trouble. She hadn't smoked since she found out she was pregnant, best part of a year ago.

'They stopped and spoke to you. I heard you talking to them. What did they say? Did they ask you about the baby?'

'What? No,' I said.

'What did they say, then?'

'Mum – what's got into you?'

Her look softened. It was the first time I'd called her that in a while.

'Sorry,' she said, blowing out a seemingly endless cloud of smoke. The smell was disgusting.

'What were they doing here?' I asked.

'They…' Her face broke – just for a moment it filled with lines, as if she would cry – then returned to normal. 'They're concerned about Sally's welfare,' she said.

'Why?'

'Because…' she drew in breath. 'Because of her leg.'

'But that was the cot, wasn't it? While she was asleep.'

She began to cry. I went over and put my arm around her and helped her sit down. The hand with the cigarette was trembling, a long piece of ash had already fallen on the vinyl floor. I took the cigarette off her and stubbed it out in the saucer she'd been using for an ashtray.

'It's all right,' I said.

'I wish your father was home,' she mumbled as she pushed her face into my blazer.

It felt weird, holding her like that.

'He'll be back soon,' I said. And then, because I couldn't think of anything else to say, I said: 'Everything will be all right.'

At that moment, I really thought it would.

'You know how much I love you, don't you, Daniel?' she said as her snuffling died down and her breathing steadied.

I didn't say anything.

'You know you mean every bit as much to me and your father as Sally, don't you?'

'Yes,' I said, because I didn't want her to keep saying things like that. I felt embarrassed.

'Good,' she said, and smiled. She continued to stare at the floor.

After what felt like a reasonable time, I stretched out my arms and released her. Then she looked up at me and smiled again.

'You really are a wonderful boy,' she said.

I nodded. 'Can I go upstairs now?' I said.

She smiled warmly at me, somehow more like a friend than a mother. It was weird, and I was pleased to get out.

When I got upstairs it was pretty dark so I switched the landing light on. The door to the cot room, nailed with a wooden giraffe saying 'Sally's Room', was ajar, and I could hear the faint rasp of the baby's breath. I went in and stood over the cot.

She was lying under a thin blue blanket. In the shadow of the bedside light her face was a hot, brownish-red, and I could see the down on her cheek and forehead. Her closed eyelids were thick, as if swollen.

I looked at the gaps in the cot's wooden slats, now lined on the inside with sheets that my parents had tied in place. They *were* wide enough for little legs to go through. It might just be possible for a baby to break a leg by accident – mightn't it?

I shuddered and looked out of the window into the spidery twigs and branches that marked the start of the wood, just across the narrow, lower section of our garden. I thought of the man, somewhere out there, sitting in his makeshift shelter, staring into the gloom, staring, staring at what?

Staring through the thicket, towards the lights of our house on the edge.

Staring through the dark trees.

At me.

10.

I got into a fight next day.

A kid in the year above me whose name I didn't know but whose acne-pitted face I did began to slap my cheek and call me names in the lunch queue. He was one of those kids everyone knew was deranged, who operated on a different plane from the rest of us. I knew he was just trying to get a rise out of me, he'd done it before.

Well, this time it worked and on the third slap I launched at him and we were soon on the ground, gasping and trying to shove each other's faces into the grey vinyl of the dining room floor. Within seconds I was being pulled off the psycho kid by Mr Slade, and moments later we were both outside the deputy head's door, fiercely not looking at each other.

I'd hoped to see Johnny after that, he always made me feel better, but I couldn't find him. So by the time the final bell went, I decided I would go see the man.

As I unlocked my bike in the school shelter I figured I'd go straight off into the woods and not even stop at home. But as I was pulling the bike out I found myself face to face with the man from the council again. He was wearing a soft black jacket today, but his eyes were still steely and green.

'Hello, Daniel.'

'Hello.'

'There's something I'd like to ask you. Would you be prepared to meet May, my colleague, and me to talk about your home?'

'What for?'

'We'd just like to make sure everything's OK for you and your sister.'

I thought for a moment. What was the right thing to do?

'OK,' I said.

'And…' he said, his eyes implying all kinds of things, '…we'd like the meeting to be just between the three of us.'

I frowned. 'You mean not tell my parents?'

He nodded but didn't say anything. Again, it was all in the eyes.

'OK,' I said.

'Our office is in the Town hall,' he said. 'On the High Street. But let's not meet there, let's meet in the café nearby, shall we? Layla's? Tomorrow, at say three-thirty after school?'

11.

After you leave the High Street on the way back it's all houses except for the one chippy on School Lane, *Mike's Fish Bar*. I was cycling past it, savouring the wafts of frying on the chilly air, when I had an idea. I stopped, chained my bike to the lamppost outside the neon-lit shopfront, and hurried inside.

Mike didn't look like a Mike at all, he was a middle-aged Asian bloke with wavy grey hair and a big, wounded nose.

'What do you like, Daniel?' he asked.

'Cod and jumbo sausage, two large chips,' I said. 'Plenty of salt and vinegar. No, make that plenty of salt and vinegar on one, and none on the other.'

'Big appetite today,' he said, snatching up his metal pincers.

Soon I was back out in the cold, pedalling furiously with the food all stuffed into my backpack, probably stinking it out, but who cared? It was a good idea. I just had to get there fast, before it got too cold.

I was cycling down the sunken track towards the old church when I saw Mr Jackson in his flat cap up ahead, walking his Labrador, Toby. Toby was hobbling a bit, probably with rheumatism or something, I thought, but then as I watched I saw he was actually doing his business, right there in the middle of the path. Mr Jackson glanced at him indifferently, then carried on walking.

'Hey!' I shouted.

He turned and faced me as I drew nearer and stopped. Toby looked up at me with a doleful expression.

'What is it?' said Mr Jackson.

'You should clear that up,' I said.

'Oh,' he said, shrugging. And then he turned and walked on.

'Hey!' I said, cycling up alongside him, slowing to his pace. 'Did you hear what I said?'

Strangely, he continued to ignore me, hunching his face into his tartan scarf and walking on, looking at the ground a few metres ahead.

'It's disgusting, leaving that around,' I said, my handlebar just missing his arm as the bike wobbled. 'I cycled in it the other day. It took ages to get it off my tyres.'

I realised he wasn't going to acknowledge my presence again. I felt a sudden, intense fury, then accelerated right in front of him making him gasp and straighten up.

I thought he might shout something after me, but he didn't. Within moments, I was off the track and heading into the darkening, deeper woods.

I cycled harder and harder, using the exertion to eat up my madness. I could deal with all that later, now I needed a clear head to talk to the man.

12.

Why do we love the smell of burning wood so much?

I thought I saw the haze of smoke against the dark, wet trunks of the trees, but it could have been a trick of the eyes in the fading light. Pretty soon I caught a glimpse of the little yellow spark of his fire. As usual I felt my gut shifting like some knackered old cement mixer filled with sludge.

But I rode on, bouncing over the root-strewn earth.

He was cross-legged on the damp ground in front of the fire, gazing absently at the flames. Behind him was what must have been his shelter – a mass of thin whips somehow suspended above the ground between two trees. He looked up at the sound of my juddering bike. Soon I was in front of him, braking too hard, almost stumbling off my bike.

'How are you?'

I didn't respond to that; I was dismounting, pulling my rucksack off, tugging frantically at the zip.

'Brought you some chips,' I said, still looking down at the zip which seemed to have got caught. 'And some cod – or sausage, whichever. Thought you must be starving…'

I glanced up at him keenly, still pulling at the zip. He looked cool, sober.

'Just – one moment…' I said. The zip was obstinate; it was not coming free. 'Hopefully… they're not – too cold… Do you like salt and vinegar?' And then I swore, because the damn thing wasn't moving at all.

'Don't worry,' he said.

'No…' Desperately, I tugged it back the other way, and suddenly it was free. 'There we go,' I said, pulling it back and quickly digging my hands into the pack. The paper felt soggy, but there was still some warmth there. Proudly, I brought the chip dinner out into what remained of the daylight.

'There we go,' I repeated. I held the bag out towards him.

He looked at me, not the packet. He didn't reach out.

There was a moment of silence. Suddenly the packet in my hands felt heavy, very heavy, so much more than a lump of greasy potato, decapitated fish, and pigs' guts.

'No,' he said quietly, and looked back at the fire.

'But… I thought you must be starving,' I said.

He continued to stare down. I could see the tiny flames reflected in his blue eyes.

'It's chips,' I said, sounding feeble. 'I bought you some chips…'

But now, like Mr Jackson, he seemed to be ignoring me. I felt a sudden, bitter pain, like a wasp sting in the throat. Tears pricked my eyes.

'Have it your way!' I cried. Feeling the injustice of it, the deep ingratitude, I flung the packet at the fire. A few chips flew free, cut golden fingers in the dimness of the forest, but the rest struck the centre of the blaze, sending sparks into the man's thick clothing.

He brushed them quickly, as I turned and sped off into the dismal woods.

13.

I got home full of a fury that I wanted Richard and Joanne to feel.

But as soon as I was in, sweating from my pedalling despite the dark and cold, I realised that – as usual – it wasn't my turn for the spotlight. Coming into the kitchen, I found Richard standing over a pan of frying burgers with a spatula wearing just his work shirt and his boxer shorts. The heat was too high and the fat was spitting up at him. Some of his hair had come out of his ponytail and was hanging long down the side of his cheeks.

'Help me with this!' he said.

'No!' I said, rushing out of the room.

'Come back!'

The door to the lounge was ajar and I could hear Sally wailing over the stern announcements of the news on TV. I could also hear Joanne, weeping softly.

I turned and headed upstairs.

14.

The next day at school things weren't much better. The kid from the year above with the acne found me at first break and tried to start a fight again, as if I'd make the same mistake twice. I got to open a conversation with Johnny by telling him about the fight, but as soon as I turned the subject on to war games and the weekend he started making excuses and telling me he was going to stay with his gran so couldn't make it.

But none of that was as bad as what happened after school.

As I came out of the main gates on my bike I noticed a huge bloke standing on the far pavement holding a smart-looking hybrid bike. He was wearing a dark suit and tie, completely at odds with his bushy brown hair and beard. He was a caveman dressed for business, and he watched me closely as I rode past him. I felt like telling him to look somewhere else, but something about him made me keep quiet.

When I got to the High Street I realised I had a few minutes before my meeting with the man and woman in the café. For a moment I wondered what to do but then I spotted a shop called *Skitter Paws* with a cardboard display of an Afghan Hound with a bone-shaped chew in its mouth and it gave me an idea. I locked my bike to some railings and hurried in.

When I came out the caveman with the suit was waiting for me. I tried to turn away and hurry for the café but he ran a couple of steps and grabbed my arm. I turned and looked up at his broad face, and saw he had sties at the corners of both eyes.

'I'll scream,' I said.

He pulled me close to his ugly face. 'Don't go near him again,' he hissed.

'What?' I said.

'Keep away from him. Or it's trouble.' He had a heavy accent, like a Brummie. I felt really scared, and wondered for a moment what he would do. I imagined him having a small, concealed blade, which I'd feel in my guts before I saw it.

'Leave me alone,' I whispered. His mouth was open and I could see his clenched yellow teeth. Some spit was dribbling into his beard. I'd never seen so much hatred in someone's eyes, so much venom – it was like they were drilling into me. I felt I was losing it, frozen and confused like a rabbit in headlights.

'Hey! Get away from him!'

I looked round and saw a young woman in pale tracksuit bottoms and a black puffer jacket. She was heading towards us, her face twisted in anger.

The man pushed me away and began to walk off. He didn't even look back at the woman, who came straight up to me.

'Are you OK, love?' She smelt of stale cigarette smoke.

I nodded, shaken.

'What was he doing?'

'I don't know,' I said. 'He just grabbed me.'

'We should get a copper,' she said, looking around.

'No,' I said. I wanted to avoid more complications. My head was feeling like it would burst.

The man got back to his bike, which he'd left propped up against a wall for anyone to steal. He turned and threw me another one of his unpleasant stares, and then cycled off.

'Are you sure?' she said. She'd fished a pink mobile from her tracksuit pocket.

'Yes,' I said. 'Look – thanks for helping, but I'm late for a meeting.'

She looked at me. How often do kids go to meetings?

'What if he comes after you again? He might be some kind of paedo,' said the woman.

'He won't,' I said, God knows why.

'How do you know?' she said.

'I don't but – look, I just have to go,' I said, and began to walk away.

She was still watching me, baffled, as I hurried up the steps into the café.

15.

'Daniel – how did you get that cut on your head?'

They both stared hard at it. This was what they had me in for; it wasn't just the baby's leg. The silence hung in the air, unearthly, like a crowd watching a man being strung up to die. For a moment, I let it hang.

'I fell off my bike,' I said softly, gazing at the varnished ridge at the edge of the table. The café was roomy, with brown walls and chattering mums with pushchairs and babies. There was a smell of damp alongside the overpowering coffee. The sharp, distracting hiss of steam.

'Where did that happen?' asked the tall woman, whose name was May. Today she was wearing a purple shawl and a white felt beret. *Indoors.*

'In the woods,' I said.

'Going too fast?' asked Paul, the man with the glasses.

'Probably.'

'Was anyone else involved?' asked May. She smiled at me. I thought she seemed a lot friendlier today than she had the first time we met.

'No.'

'When did it happen?' said Paul.

'Last Saturday.'

'Before the baby broke her leg,' said May.

I nodded at the double act.

A pause, then Paul said:

'Are you happy at the moment Daniel?'

I shrugged.

'How's the atmosphere at home?'

Pause.

'Daniel?'

'A bit stressful,' I said. 'Mum's always with the baby and Dad keeps complaining he doesn't get any sleep.'

'And what about you? Do you get enough sleep?'

'I suppose.'

'Things are hard with a new baby around,' said May. 'Tensions rise. It can be hard on everyone.'

'Yes.'

I looked up and caught them sharing a glance.

'And the baby,' said May, smiling. 'How do you feel about the baby?'

'She's my sister,' I said. I didn't know where they were going now. I started to feel uneasy. 'Why do you have to ask all these questions?'

'Like I said at the beginning,' said Paul, 'we're here to help you. We have to make sure everything is OK in your home, and you're the best person for us to ask. There's probably a completely normal reason for Sally's broken leg – but in these cases, when it's difficult to tell, we must do all we can to be sure.'

I frowned.

'Do you have any relatives that you see a lot of? Anyone who comes to stay with you?'

'Why?'

'One thing we can do is ask your parents to invite a close relative in at times like this. Someone who can make sure everything is safe.'

'Safe?'

'Yes. That you and your sister are safe.'

I thought for a moment. This was certainly something I hadn't expected.

'There's my grandpa. Grandpa Bob.'

'How old is he?'

'I don't know. Eighty?'

'Would you like it if Grandpa Bob came to stay with you for a while?' said May.

It felt odd, having a complete stranger ask me a question like that. I shrugged.

'Is that a yes or a no shrug?'

'I suppose so. Yes,' I said. It made some sense.

'OK. We'll see what we can do. But for now, here's our numbers.' She passed me their cards with their names and job titles and mobile numbers, as well as an out-of-hours number.

'You can call us anytime you feel like it during the daytime in the week, or call the other number if it's at night or on the weekend,' said Paul, the Closer. 'Anytime. You can obviously talk to your parents about this meeting, but… we suggest you don't as it might cause unnecessary stress.' He glanced again at May and I thought he looked a little uncertain. 'We hope you understand,' he added.

'Yes.'

'And we might contact you again at some stage – I hope that's all right?' He seemed strangely keen.

'Yes,' I said.

I noticed May was looking at me very closely. Her eyes were hooded, full of concern. Then she said something strange:

'We wouldn't normally do something like this, Daniel. Meet you by yourself in a café. But we have a feeling and… we care about you. Daniel, we really do…'

I looked at her for a moment then said:

'Can I go now?'

16.

'Hold her leg carefully!'

'I am!'

'Watch out for her hands!'

'Stop shouting!'

It was Saturday, Richard and Joanne were changing Sally's nappy on a mat on the kitchen table, and Johnny was with his 'relatives'. The baby was screaming, the loudest, shrillest noise a human being can make, I should know. Her whole being was consumed by abject misery, because she didn't like being manipulated.

I had to get out.

'Grandpa Bob will be here at 3.30,' said Joanne as I opened the back door. Richard, holding the baby's legs, scowled. 'Make sure you're back to see him for tea,' Joanne finished.

Sometime later that afternoon, I was standing in my saddle at the top of a slope when I heard Mr Jackson calling for his dog in the woods. I watched as he came in sight on the mushy path below me. He was wearing his flat cap and his breath was steaming in the cold. I was warm from all my activity.

'Toby!'

He shouted, squelching in the mud in his walking boots. 'Toby!'

Suddenly he looked up and saw me. The immediate hostility in his expression quickly turned to hope.

'Have you seen my dog?' he called.

'No,' I said.

'He ran off down by the bridge,' he said.

I nodded and turned my bike. 'If I see him I'll try and bring him back,' I said. 'I know where you live.'

'Yes – thank you,' said the old man. 'Thank you,' he repeated, and walked off.

His frantic calls were soon muted by the forest. The only sounds I could hear were my own, the swishing of my wheels through leaf mould, my deep, steady breathing. I cycled to my jumps, ran them a few times, then headed back to the man's den with a lump in my throat.

He was starting to look a whole lot thinner. And whiter, if that was possible.

'I'm sorry about the other day,' I said, stopping in front of his fire.

He watched me carefully, looking up from the book he was reading.

'I'm having a bad time at the moment. Can I talk to you?'

He made the slightest nod. I stood my bike against a tree and sat down beside him. He was perched on a stump, but I had to sit on the damp ground and look up at the side of his face.

'Do you think there's something bad about this place?' I said, staring at the flames. 'Something bad about these woods?'

'Yes.'

'So do I.'

The fire spat. A curl of smoke wound upwards against the greyness of the trees.

'My sister's got a broken leg, and social services think my parents did it.'

There, it was said. I held my breath, waiting for his response.

When none came I said: 'Do you care?'

'You know I care,' he said. His voice was soft but deep, the kind of voice you could feel all the way through you.

'Supposing it's true? Supposing they did do it?' I said. 'What if I'm living with child abusers?'

He shook his head, looked at the fire. His beard looked dark, almost black, on his cheeks.

'I'm adopted, you know,' I said. And then added: 'I don't know what to do.'

'You do,' he said.

I looked up and around at the thousand black branches clawing the sky. Despite the fire I shivered.

'What are the rules?' I said.

'You tell me,' he said.

'OK,' I said, perching on the balls of my feet and leaning into the fire. 'You have to live out here on your own for a set time without any help from the outside world. And you can drink but you can't eat anything. At all. Is that it?'

He smiled ruefully.

'That's why you wouldn't eat the chips, right?'

'Yes.'

'How long are you doing it for?'

'Until April.'

'You sure you'll make it?'

'I'll survive.'

'Why?'

'Why what?'

'Why are you doing it?'

'Because it helps me.'

'Helps you how?'

'Helps me prepare.'

'For what?'

'For all that's coming.'

I sat back on the ground.

'That sounds serious,' I said. 'You don't say much, do you?' I added, when it was clear he wasn't going to elaborate.

'There's no need, is there?' he said.

'That's bleak,' I said.

'There's always hope,' he said.

'Hope,' I said, then added: 'Do you want to go and see the old folly with me? One day next week? You can climb up and get a wicked view.'

17.

The next day, Sunday, I was woken by a light knock on my bedroom door.

I peered up from under my quilt, my head dull with sleep. I'd been dreaming, but the fleeting images vanished before I could grab them.

Joanne poked her head round the door. 'We're going to church, Daniel,' she said. 'Do you want to come?'

I wrinkled my nose. 'Not really,' I said.

'We thought… we want to say some prayers,' she said. 'For Sally.'

'Say one for me,' I said, yawning. 'I'm really tired, though. I need a lie-in.'

'OK,' she said. 'We'll be back at eleven-thirty.'

She closed the door and I slumped over on to my back, shutting my eyes again. I could hear the birds chirping outside and light was filtering through the curtains. I thought about how relieved I was that Joanne hadn't insisted on me going.

That was one thing I really respected her and Richard for. They both knew that from an early age I'd had my doubts about God. I'd always wondered, what was the point in going to church and praying if God still let terrible tragedies and natural disasters happen? Why did He save some but not others, others who were often more deserving? He could surely stop all this trouble brewing in the Middle East if He wanted to, couldn't He? I know there's all those clever arguments about free will, us being allowed to go our own way etcetera – but for me, that's all they are. Clever arguments, used by vicars and priests to justify their position.

If He still makes the good suffer, what's the point in Him?

No, church wasn't for me, and thankfully Joanne and Richard gave me the space to have my own opinions.

I heard the thump of the door closing below, the rumble of Grandpa Bob's voice as they headed out the garden to the car. The opening and closing of the car doors, the engine coughing into life, the short squeal of the fanbelt as they drove off down the road.

Alone. I was alone.

What to do with the day? I realised I wasn't going back to sleep now. I thought about the man, wanted desperately to go and see him – but thought better of it. I couldn't pester him all the time. He'd said he'd go to the folly with me next week. So I had to think of something else to do.

I looked at my desk, saw the scattered legions of orcs, elves, ogres and wraiths waiting.

That was it, decided. A day of painting lay ahead.

18.

'Did you manage to catch up on your sleep at the weekend, Mr Page?'

One of the things I liked about Miss Hailey was the way she teased us, calling us all by our surnames. It made you feel like you could trust her.

'Yes, thank you, Miss,' I replied with a flourish. I'm not one of those kids who minds being singled out.

'Good. So, last week we were talking about Islam. This week, in the true contradictory spirit of the humanities, we're going to talk about silence.'

I laughed, and a few of the kids – including that prude, Gemma Tees – threw crazy looks at me. I realised most of them were so dim they didn't get it. I was pleased to see Johnny give me a knowing smile, though. Even if he was sitting by Gemma. I'd get to him as soon as the lesson finished.

'Let's start with a simple question,' said Miss Hailey, wandering up to the whiteboard and unclicking the cap of her marker.

She spoke and wrote: 'WHY?' Then turned back to face us.

'One of the most fundamental questions we can ask,' she said. 'Somebody give me a 'why' question, please.'

'Why do we have to go to school?' said Sean Coulton.

A few people groaned at his obviousness.

'Why do we have to go to school?' repeated Miss Hailey. 'Good question. Who has an answer?'

'Because we have to learn things,' said Gemma, slouching back and raising her eyes.

'Why?' said Miss Hailey.

'Because we need grades to go to university,' said Bill Evans. Everyone called him Narna Bill because he always had two bananas in his packed lunch. Kids are so imaginative.

'Why?' said Miss Hailey. I could see where she was going.

'Because we have to get a good job…'

'Why?'

'Because we don't want to go on benefits…'

'Why?'

'Because then we'd be like Matthew's dad!'

The class laughed as Matthew Jonson's cheeks burned.

'That's enough,' said Miss Hailey, and everyone went quiet. The silence hung in the air. She was one of those teachers who could hold your attention.

'"Why" is one of those questions you can keep asking,' she said at last. 'You can imagine our ancestors sitting in the cave entrance gazing up at the stars and asking the same thing. It never ends.

'Except in silence.

'And that's the conclusion that many of our religious traditions have come to, when it comes to contemplating the big questions about the meaning of life. Eventually all explanations – all words, in fact – reach limits and we're left in a quiet state of wonder at the mystery of things.'

I thought about that.

'…again, Mr Page?' I guessed from the way she was looking at me I'd been away with the fairies again. It's OK for it to happen once – but twice means sustained ribbing.

The class was laughing.

'Yes, sorry Miss,' I said.

'Don't worry,' she said, but I could see a shadow of doubt on her face. Did I look tired? I sure wasn't sleeping much, with the baby crying and everything on my mind.

After the class I ran up and literally pulled Johnny away from Gemma.

'Come on,' I said, 'I need to talk.'

He looked very uncertain but let me take him away. Gemma threw me daggers.

'You've got to let me in again, Johnny,' I said.

'Never knew I'd locked you out,' he said.

'Come on,' I said.

He shrugged.

'I need a friend to talk to,' I said. 'Everything's gone mad in my life.'

'How?'

'My sister broke her leg in the night. My parents took her to hospital and they've set social services on to it, saying it's suspicious circumstances. I got interviewed by two social workers! They've made my Grandpa come and live with us to make sure we're safe. They've turned my family into spies on one another.'

I could see from his look he was impressed.

'That really is mad,' he said. 'Nuclear weapons in the Middle East, famine in Africa, Mr Morris's son topping himself and now this – everything's falling apart at the seams! But Richard and Joanne wouldn't do anything like that to Sally,' he added. Because I called them by their Christian names he did too.

'I know,' I said. 'It must have been an accident. But you know how it is in the papers these days. All those councils being sued because they didn't do the right thing. They have to take precautions.'

'Wow!' he said. 'So they sent your Grandpa to stay with you?'

'Yeah,' I said.

'How long for?'

'We don't know. Until they're happy that we're safe. They're visiting Joanne every few days. It's freaking her out.'

'I bet. Why did they interview you?'

'Because I had a cut on my head from falling off my bike. They thought Richard and Joanne did that too.'

'Shit!'

'Even when I told them, I'm not sure they believed me.'

'Wow!' He couldn't stop exclaiming. We were nearly at the Maths block for next class, so I realised I had to seize my moment.

'What are you doing this weekend?'

'I don't know.'

'Will you come round for a battle?'

He looked uncertain. 'No, Dan,' he said.

'Come on, Johnny! It's not that bad in the house and I've got the dark elves painted. Two new battalions!'

'No, I don't think I can.'

'Why not?'

'You know why not.'

19.

I have a temper on me. Sometimes I see red.

That's why Johnny doesn't want to play with me again. It's nothing to do with his getting into girls, nothing to do with Gemma Tees. It's because last time we had a battle I lost and threw my ogre centurion across the room at him. And it cut the top of his head.

It's easy to make excuses. My life – my whole existence in fact – has been hard. As for my family... *well*.

I shouldn't have done it. And now I'd lost my only true friend.

20

Grandpa Bob was in his black felt hat planting bulbs in the garden when I got home that evening. He was sniffing heavily and wiping his nose with his sleeve. The sky was overcast and it felt like it was going to get dark early.

'Brittle bone disease,' he said, tugging at a thin root as I wheeled my bike up to him.

'What?'

'Your sister has brittle bone disease,' he said. 'She thrashes around in her sleep, gets her leg caught in the crib, and breaks it herself. But no baby breaks her bones in a crib normally, everyone knows babies' bones are bendy like new tree roots.' He pulled the root up from the ground like the string of a bow. It was covered in frail shaggy hairs.

'She breaks it because she has brittle bone disease.'

I'd never heard of it, but it was one of those things you didn't need to ask what it meant.

'What makes you think that?' I asked.

He stood up straight and stretched his back. He was wearing his old blue Barbour and a pair of Joanne's yellow rubber cleaning gloves.

'Used to know someone who had it,' he said. 'He was a soldier. It was undiagnosed for years. One day he was on an assault course, jumped off a section of rigging, and broke both his femurs.'

'Wow,' I said. Grandpa Bob had been in the army once – a long time ago. Most of his life he'd worked as an electrician.

'Bloody doctors,' he said. 'They send for the social workers before they even think about doing their own jobs.'

'What do you mean?'

'They should have bloody tested her there and then. Not leapt to stupid conclusions. As if Joanne – or Richard, for that matter – could ever do that to their own child!'

'So what are we going to do?' I asked.

'Get them to do their jobs,' he said. 'I'm going to buy a video camera with a night light, set it up above her cot. That way we can prove how much she moves in the night. And at the same time we're going to take her back and demand that they do whatever tests they have to.

'We're not having something like this left hanging over us,' he continued. 'It'll eat away at us over the years. We're going to get it cleared up.'

In a swift movement he raised the spade then plunged it into the ground.

Looking down I saw he'd severed the root in two.

21.

Grandpa Bob cooked dinner that night.

I sat in the kitchen half-surfing the web and half-watching him make up the Spanish omelette, frying peppers, garlic, onions, and potato, adding paprika, salt and pepper, pouring on the beaten egg-and-milk gloop. It sizzled and smelt good, much better than the second-rate burgers, fish fingers and frozen pizzas Richard had been cooking for the last couple of weeks.

It took forever to get Joanne into the kitchen when the omelette was ready. She'd taken to spending her whole time with the baby, even sitting beside her whilst she was asleep. She was terrified something bad would happen to her if she left her on her own.

When Richard finally led her in, holding her by the arm, she didn't look at all well. Her face was drawn and white, and she had a funny way of looking at us – like she didn't want us to notice her, she looked away quickly every time you caught her eye. Something was clearly going wrong inside her. She was worrying too much, and it created an atmosphere that lasted throughout the meal. That, combined with the fact that Grandpa Bob and Richard didn't get on.

'I couldn't believe Distribution today,' said Richard, buttering a slice of bread. 'Last month I told them to make sure they got enough of the new Moonlite trainer in. Everyone knew they'd be selling like hotcakes, after the funny cow ad. Eighty thousand, I told them, with three-quarters going to the northern stores. How many do you think they got in?'

'Do tell,' said Grandpa Bob.

Richard glanced suspiciously at him before saying: 'Three thousand. I've had non-stop complaints from store managers. Head of Distribution is blaming one of her middle managers, but that's what she always does. I'm going to have to speak to the SMT. I think it's time we got her out…'

'Don't go getting into trouble,' said Joanne.

Richard looked at her. 'How would I get into trouble?'

'Like you did last time, with Ben and Pete.'

Richard blanched. 'That was a long time ago, Jo,' he said.

'We don't want you going to prison again. Not with the baby ill.'

You don't realise how much noise and movement goes into a family eating its dinner until it stops.

It was Grandpa Bob who broke the silence. 'You've nearly finished now, love,' he said. 'I'll make you a cup of tea and we'll go and sit by the fire.'

'I need to go and check the baby.'

I thought how she'd always referred to Sally by her name before.

'OK, we'll do it together,' said Grandpa Bob.

'No – I'll take her,' said Richard, standing up. I caught a glimpse of fire in the look the two men exchanged, and then Richard was leading Joanne out of the room.

Grandpa Bob and I sat in silence, staring after them. Then he said:

'Come on, Dan, finish your tea.'

I nodded. 'Will she be all right?' I said.

'Once we've cleared everything up,' he said. 'I'm going to order that camera later. And I'll call the doctor's tomorrow, to get those tests done.'

After a moment he said: 'She'll be all right.'

22.

For three-and-a-half years Joanne and I had lived alone in the house, from when I was six to just short of my tenth birthday.

Of course when Richard first left us I was just told that he was going to live in another house for a while. It had nothing to do with the fact he didn't love me or Joanne. We would be able to see him, but only once or twice a month in a special room. At the time that seemed exotic and intriguing. Did other people's fathers stay in special rooms?

I remember having a vague sense of him having done something that other people didn't think was the right thing to do. This was given poignancy one night when I couldn't sleep and came downstairs in my pyjamas only to overhear a relative – an older female cousin of Joanne's, who was spicy and wore a lot of makeup – laughing and telling her mum that Richard 'always believed he was brighter than he was and thought he could get away with it.' Now I think back on it, I'm sure she must have been drunk. There was something else that she said which gave me the impression that Richard had taken something that wasn't his.

On the day after my eighth birthday Joanne took me for a walk in the woods on a frosty morning to tell me Richard had tried to use a computer in his job to pay two other men – now I think they might have been called Ben and Josh – more money than they had really earned from the company he worked for.

'Was that like stealing money from the company?' I'd asked.

'Yes, that's right,' she said. 'But he won't do it again.'

'How do you know?' I said.

'Because now he's been to prison so he knows it's wrong.'

'Is that the only way you know if something's wrong?' I said.

'No,' said Joanne, acting strangely. 'You know because… because your conscience tells you.'

'Then why didn't Richard's conscience tell him it was wrong?'

'It probably did,' she said. 'But he didn't listen to it properly. He wanted more money to help us as a family – but he went about it the wrong way.'

I don't remember the day he came out of prison, but I do remember after a short period of happiness how hard things were for a while as he tried to find another job. Because he'd used to work managing the money of businesses he couldn't use his old skills, so he had to look for different types of jobs. It was the summer holidays and each day he would put on a suit and take me with him as he trawled industrial estates and shops asking for work. Occasionally someone would offer him a proper interview, but as soon as they'd found out he'd been to prison they turned him down. Then he'd be back home, arguing half the night with Joanne. It was Grandpa Bob, fretting about me and Joanne, who eventually asked one of his closest friends who worked for a famous high street sports shop if he could give Richard an administrative post in the Head Office.

I think that was why Grandpa Bob didn't really like him much.

23.

I was surprised to see the man there when I went to the folly after school the next day. I'd told him where it was the week before, but we hadn't arranged a time to meet or anything.

He was waiting by the doorway, his breath steaming around his shaggy beard. It was cold.

'How are you?' I said, as I skidded to a stop a couple of feet in front of him, the back wheel swinging out and round.

He nodded. 'I'm all right,' he said.

'All right,' I said, smiling, as I eased my bike to the ground. 'Come on, let's go up!' I was excited. I liked showing people things and places I knew well. And – who knew what might happen?

The folly was built on the brow of a hill in the woods. It was only a little hill, cleared near the top, with a semi-circle of trees in a thick cluster at the rear of the old building. The folly had been built out of large brown stones, lined by a bright ochre cement. I always thought there was something disturbing about the stones, their odd, bulgy shapes somehow reminding me of the flashes you saw at the back of your eyes when you'd knocked your head. They were ugly stones, interrupted by neat rust-coloured bricks that knitted the corners of the hexagonal folly together. The windows, alternating in a diagonal pattern up the walls, were just thin slits, like narrowed eyes. It was a weird building, that's what I'm saying.

And I knew how to get in it.

I almost took his hand, his dirt-encrusted fingertips, then decided against it, instead beckoning him to follow. He did, still with that inscrutable look on his face. I could see the dryness of his skin, the lines there, lines of age, possibly sorrow. Or maybe he'd smiled and laughed too much in his life. I'm not so good at reading faces, I don't always get it right.

At the back we found the rotted wooden door that was barred and chained. It looked impenetrable, but of course it wasn't. The padlock had been smashed for months, probably by some kid with an iron pipe, and no one had replaced it. I tugged the chain free and then lifted the wooden bar. A quick shove and the door swung inward on the damp dark.

'Come on,' I said. 'It's safe.'

He followed me in, stooping a little to pass beneath the arch of the doorway. Inside it was close, gritty, smelling of old stone, not piss, thankfully. All there was to see were the steps leading up around a central pillar and some mud and gravel on the floor. There weren't even any crisp packets or plastic bottles. I didn't reckon anyone else knew it was open.

'Why do you think they built this?' I asked, when we started up the stairs.

'I don't know,' he said.

Man of many words.

It was tough getting to the top, I could cycle for hours on end but give me seventy steps and I was hurting for breath. For a while all there was was the steady strike of our shoes on worn stone, an unpleasant sound like the hiss of hot iron in cold water.

We were probably two-thirds of the way up when I stopped, panting, and reached out for the wall.

'Just got to get my breath,' I said.

He waited behind me. I could hear him too, breathing sharply through his nostrils.

'You're a lot fitter than me,' I said.

'Am I?'

'Perhaps.'

A little while later a brightness grew above and then we were through an even smaller doorway and standing on the roof, the parapet waist-high all around us.

'Come on, the views are great,' I said.

I went over to the edge and looked down the hill. The trees started towards the bottom, lots of pines with some oaks and sycamore. They carried on for what looked like miles before you could see open fields. There were a few clusters of houses that way, villages, maybe a town or two in the far distance. Abingale was out of sight, somewhere on our right.

'What do you think?' I said, looking at the side of his face. The wind was blowing free a few bits of his hair that weren't too greasy. I could see into his beard, the black and grey in there amid the gingery brown.

'It's a good view,' he said.

I looked at him expectantly. It wasn't just a good view. It was a *great* view.

I felt something growing inside me as he continued to watch the trees below, to scan the shades of grey in the cloud, the land beyond. Anger.

'Come on,' I said. 'It's better than that. Aren't you pleased I brought you up here?'

Do you know what he did then? He only went and winced.

'Look,' I said. 'I've been trying to get through to you ever since I met you. But you're not giving me anything. I'm finding it all so…'

'I don't owe you anything,' he said.

'Did I say you did?'

'No.'

I grabbed the top of one of the castellations, breathing heavily. 'Sometimes I get really… desperate,' I said the last word quietly. 'I could almost…'

I looked down sharply, at the ground fifty foot below. I turned to him and he was watching me carefully now.

'What's the point of all this?' I said. 'Life, I mean…'

His pale blue eyes.

'You've got problems too, I can tell,' I said.

Watching.

'Why don't we… why don't we just bloody… just bloody *jump* and be done with it all!'

I really felt it then, the whole damned burden.

My head hung low between my shoulders and I watched him out of the corner of my eye.

He didn't move, not even an outstretched hand. He'd been on all those campaigns against war, cruelty, injustice but now I wondered… did he ever really care? Was it all about the image?

I swung round to face him. 'Come on, let's do it! Jump with me! Perhaps some guardian angel might save us. And if they don't, what have we lost?'

'Thank you for bringing me up here,' he said.

Then turned, ducked under the doorway, and began to make his way back down the stairs.

24.

I was so depressed when I got home.

To make it worse, Richard and Joanne were in a full-blown argument over something to do with a card and stamps. When I came in from the dark, the shouts faded quickly and I heard Joanne begin to sob in the dining room. I hung up my coat on the kitchen wall and fidgeted for a moment. Our house is long and thin and you have to go through the dining room to get anywhere else. I was reaching for the door handle, Joanne still sobbing and Richard speaking to her quietly, when Grandpa Bob came in from the other side. He must have walked right past them.

'Daniel, are you going to help me put the camera up?' he said.

'What?' I said. 'It's arrived already?'

He nodded, his lips quivering a little, like they could turn into a scowl or a grin.

'Come on,' he said and led me past a flush-cheeked Richard, standing at the edge of the dining table, over which Joanne was part leaning, part sprawled. Neither of them said anything as Grandpa Bob took me through. They just watched me quietly. The baby was asleep in the Moses basket in the corner of the room.

'What were they arguing about?' I asked, as we climbed the steep narrow steps to the landing.

'Just a card,' said Grandpa Bob. 'One of Richard's friends passed away. Don't let it trouble you, Dan, there's a lot on their minds.'

The box with the camera was in the baby's room. Grandpa Bob had already opened it and the cables were out but not the camera itself. It was still housed in its polystyrene casing. It was a green thing, camouflaged, about the size of a bible.

'It's made for shooting wildlife in your garden at night,' he said. 'Get it out.'

I prised it from its squeaky case and looked at it. 'Will it work indoors?'

'Same principle,' he said. 'As soon as a little critter moves it turns on.'

'We'll have to put it outside next,' I said. 'After we've used it for Sally, I mean. We can see if there's any foxes or badgers in the garden.'

'Yes indeedy,' he said. 'I'm sure there will be.'

We tried a few places for it then realised it would be best on the ceiling, facing down at her.

'How are we going to fix it up?' I asked.

Grandpa Bob looked at the Artex ceiling, thinking. 'Duct tape,' he said eventually.

'It'll fall off on her, won't it?' I said.

'Not if we use enough,' he said. 'And we won't put it directly over her.'

'Joanne won't like it.'

He went downstairs and a short while later came back with a roll of the thick silver tape. As he began to tape it up, there wasn't much for me to do except watch him and think about the man in the woods.

25.

The next morning I wanted to watch the footage but as usual the chaos in the house prevented me having any time with the adults.

Richard, late for work, knocked one of those four-pint cartons of milk across the kitchen table when he was gulping orange juice. Joanne insisted on clearing it up, shoving him aside and leaving a wailing Sally for Grandpa Bob to deal with. I tried to ask Grandpa Bob if we could get the camera down but he in turn brushed me off, telling me he'd do it later.

I peeked into Sally's room after I'd brushed my teeth and saw it up there, still firmly suspended from the ceiling with the duct tape. It hadn't budged an inch. Which was a good thing, even though Grandpa Bob had ended up putting it well away from the baby's body. My best guess was that it would have hit the bottom left-hand corner of the cot if it had fallen in the night. Well away from Sally, unless it bounced on to her after striking the wood. Grandpa Bob had insisted it would still switch on if she moved, she was well within its activation zone. The distance from Sally's little body was the only reason Joanne had agreed to it being fixed up there like that. That, and the fact it might get social services off their backs, of course.

I left for school on my bike feeling miserable and as usual right at the bottom of the pecking order. Sometimes it felt like I was invisible.

I was so caught up in it all that I didn't notice the social worker lady, May, outside the school gate, not until she stepped up in front of me and spoke.

'Hello, Daniel.'

I stopped pedalling and dismounted.

'Hello, May.'

'Has your grandpa come yet?'

'Yes, he's been here for days.'

'Oh good. I've…' I noticed her eyes flick away, up towards the stone plaque carved with the school name above the doors. Was she nervous? 'I've been worried about you,' she said.

I nodded.

'You're OK?'

'Yes.'

'We – Paul and I – we realise we shouldn't quite be speaking to you like this, without your parents around but…'

'Grandpa Bob put a camera up last night in the baby's room,' I said, as much to relieve the tension as anything. 'One of those wildlife cameras that go on when something moves. He thinks it will show if she wriggles around. Show if she might have had an accident, done it herself.'

'What a good idea,' said May. She had a different coloured beret on today. It was blue.

We stood there for a moment, I watched Jo Davidson go past wheeling his scooter and giving us comedy goggle eyes.

'I need to go in,' I said.

'Yes – of course you do.' She looked at me again with pained eyes. 'You're… such a quiet child. Sensitive. You know you can call me anytime. Anytime you're worried. About anything.' She said *anything* with emphasis and reached towards my hand. I moved it away. I frowned then stopped and remembered to smile.

'Thank you,' I said, and walked past her and through the gates. Mr Brady, the Year 7 History teacher with the dark tache and the little hazel eyes, gave me an odd look, something in between a grin and a leer.

Sometimes grown-ups can be very strange.

26.

I was straight into the woods again that evening after school. I wanted to see him, see how he was after the folly.

As I approached his makeshift camp, slipping about through the mud, I became aware of a crashing sound and then something fast was coming at me from the side. There was a lot of loudness and I tumbled sideways, bumping the ground hard with my shoulder and crying out in pain.

There was snarling and I realised that the black dog was trying to get to me but being slowed down by the fallen bike.

And then there was another shape behind it in the trees, lunging and snatching it by the collar.

The man, pulling back the dog.

'Stop now, there, calm down,' he was saying. 'Steady…'

Propped up on an elbow, I realised it was Toby, Mr Jackson's dog. With a rag on the side of its head, somehow held in place so it didn't fall off.

Toby was snarling at me but the man had a good hold of it.

'Scared the life out of me!' I cried, clambering to my feet.

The man knelt beside it, holding it around the neck. The dog became quiet.

'That's Mr Jackson's dog,' I said. 'Toby. He lost it the other day.'

'I found him a few hundred yards away,' said the man. 'He was whimpering at the bottom of a bank. His head was injured.'

I frowned. 'Weird.'

'I used a bit of my shirt to make a compress,' said the man. 'Tied it on with one of my boot laces.'

'From the way he attacked me, I wonder if he's got a brain injury?' I said. 'Brain damage can make dogs – any animal, really – more aggressive, can't it?'

'Yes,' said the man.

'I came out to say sorry for the other day,' I blurted.

He looked at me, still kneeling by the dog, which was looking sorrowfully down at the ground and licking his hand now.

'I don't know what got into me,' I said. 'At the folly. All that talk about what does life mean, and… jumping.'

'It's nothing,' said the man.

'Have you read that kid's book, Skellig?' I said.

'What?'

'Skellig. We did it at school.'

'No,' he said.

'It's just… it's about a boy who finds a man in his shed. He looks after him and he's this kind of… angel-bird thing.'

The man raised his eyebrows.

'You don't say much, do you?' I said.

'No, I don't.'

I watched Toby licking his hand. The expression on the dog's face as it licked was strangely docile, enraptured. Like some kind of supplicant.

'Do you want me to take him back to his owner?' I said. 'Now he's calmed down a bit.'

The man looked down at the dog. He lifted the rag on its head a little and peered underneath.

'He needs a vet,' he said. 'OK.'

He gave me the lead and with a couple of tugs and *come on, Tobys* I finally managed to get him trotting behind me as I cycled away.

27.

'Look – there! Look how she's kicking! It's like she's at a bleedin' rodeo or something…'

It was an electric moment in the house. We were all – Richard, Joanne with Sally at her breast, Grandpa Bob and me – sitting around the laptop at the kitchen table, watching the camera footage.

'You're right,' said Richard, his face far too close against the screen. I could see the brightness of the image reflected on his cheeks and in tiny grids on his eyes. His ponytail was swishing a bit close to my face so I slid sideways along the bench against Joanne's arm, which was holding the baby.

And Grandpa Bob was right. The first night Sally had remained under her lacy yellow blanket but on the second – and especially the third, which was what we were watching now – she had pushed free of it and begun to writhe and roll all over the place. In several sections of footage, her grey-and-white little body came right up against the side of the cot, which was now protected by heavy duty blankets tucked in the mattress and fixed around the end posts with cable ties. She even kicked at it a few times.

'Game, set and match,' said Richard, grinning and turning towards Joanne.

She smiled wanly back at him. There was a red mark on the side of her cheek which I thought might be a massing boil but I didn't like to look at it too long.

'It's nothing conclusive,' she said.

'This is going to sort it out for sure,' said Grandpa Bob. I suspected he hadn't heard her, he didn't listen so well. 'I'm going to call those social service do-gooders right away.'

'I suppose I better do it,' said Richard.

'It's not conclusive,' Joanne said again. I glanced at her then looked away quickly. I was too close to the boil.

'We've got to try, love,' said Grandpa Bob.

Richard was already disappearing out the door to get some quiet to make the call.

'I'll put the kettle on,' said Grandpa Bob. 'I picked up a Swiss roll in the Coop earlier, and this deserves a celebration!'

I heard Joanne sigh. I looked at the baby and her eyes flickered open, blue and briefly observant. I tried to smile but it was hard to.

Grandpa Bob was literally bobbing with excitement as he made the tea and got the cake out the cupboard. I wasn't feeling hungry so decided to slip out and head upstairs to my room.

Richard wasn't in the dining room, nor our tiny hall, but as I put my foot on the first step I heard him speaking behind the shut door of the lounge.

'…yeah, he's… he's a little odd…'

My cheeks flushed. Was he talking about me? If he was, he was a fine one to talk.

I wanted to hang around and see if I could hear anything else, but then the dining room door opened and Joanne appeared too, perhaps coming to listen in on Richard's conversation with social services. She met my eyes before I hurried upstairs to my room.

28.

It was pouring with rain, the woods were drenching.

He wasn't eating anything.

It was pouring with rain and it was cold and he wasn't eating anything. No wonder he was ill.

I picked my way through the mulch to where he was lying on his side, his thick coat and hair saturated and darkened by the rain. He wasn't moving at all. For a moment, I wondered if this might be it.

Was he dead?

I peered over his thick clumps of hair to see the side of his face. It looked small, white and blotchy. Sallow, was that the word? His eyes were shut.

Carefully, slightly worried – I'd not been this close to him before – I knelt beside him, my knee soaking immediately in the glistening soil. The ground smelled strongly of leaf and mould, earthy, metallic, slightly uric. I realised the latter was probably him. Reflexively, I pinched my nostrils.

I opened my mouth to ask him if he was all right then stopped.

This was my chance to look at him. Really look at him, for the first time ever.

His face was so cold and pale you could see one of his veins on his forehead, bluish and thick as a shoelace. His beard as I've mentioned was not all chestnut, there was black and grey in there, some dark brown. I didn't like seeing the hair coming out of the flesh, though. It made me think of one of those David Attenborough programmes, when something unnatural and brittle, something parasitic, insect-like, erupts from something soft and yielding. Like those urban myths that got passed around school, of a wasp or spider laying eggs under your skin and them hatching later, fully formed. His eyelashes weren't much better, although at least they were nicely shaped and even. There were a few small freckles or moles on his temple, one particularly dark and with a black hair in the middle of it. It was the kind I thought you might be supposed to check with a doctor. His nose was thin and I could hear his breath whistling faintly there.

So he was alive.

Alive, but, at the end of the day, just a man. Just an innocent man.

Tentatively, I reached out and, first lightly, then more forcefully, pushed his shoulder.

He groaned.

I pushed again, cold splats of rain hitting the back of my hand.

'Come on,' I said. 'You've got to wake up.'

He said something quietly, I didn't hear.

'Wake up,' I said. His teeth were beige, like a smoker's, his lips thin, colourless.

'Leave,' he said, opening his eyes.

'Do you want anything?' I said. 'You're ill.'

'Just leave…'

Again, I felt the flash of anger. He was probably the most ungrateful person I'd ever met. Before I said something I'd regret, I stood up and marched back to my bike.

He could die there, for all I cared.

29.

On the way home, I was lucky.

I had taken to getting off my bike and walking up and over the bank of trees that faced our house on the edge of the common, as opposed to cycling the final stretch of the path that joined the road outside our house. It was just a hunch, but I was glad I'd been following it.

Because *he* was there.

The big man with the woolly beard and the bike and the Brummie accent. But this time he wasn't in his suit, he was wearing grey waterproofs because of the rain. He was standing clutching his handlebars, watching our garden. And there was another man with him. Another cyclist, an older guy with round, Harry Potter glasses and a wispy beard. He too stood by his bike, his face sheltered from the wet by a small peak cap in the hood of his khaki windcheater.

I was so glad I'd thought ahead. And so glad they hadn't seen me.

But what was I going to do?

I thought for a moment. The rain was crashing down on the trees and mulch which was good because it meant they hadn't heard me but bad because I couldn't hear what they were saying to each other and I wanted to. They both looked serious, grim, but not aggressive. Hopefully not violent. But that man, the bearded Wookiee, he'd really frightened me in town. What could he do to me?

I came up with a plan. It wasn't guaranteed to work but it was all I could think of. I set the bike down carefully on the bank and retreated slowly back from the barrier of trunks and scrub through which they could have seen me, if they'd been looking. Then I scurried back up the track to the point where an old tree with a black hole in its trunk like a gaping maw held together the bank with exposed, serpentine roots. I used them to scramble up to the top again. I was basically back on the same bank opposite the house but now so deep in scrub they wouldn't be able to see me. I picked my way upwards, taking care not to slip on the drenched mud in my school shoes.

Soon I was up much higher, on the level with our roof which I could see through the trunks. I could also see the two cyclists in the road below, far enough away that they would be unlikely to look up this high. Why would they?

I think I've already told you that our garden is flat at the front of the house but rises steeply at the side and back, with a diagonal flight of wooden steps to the top lawn. This lawn – which is a bugger to mow, I should know as I have to carry the mower up from the shed every fortnight in summer – it's protected from the encroachment of the wood by an old, unpainted picket fence. I reached this now, reached the very last section, which was out of sight of the front of the house where the men waited.

It was easy to clamber over. I then hurried down the short lawn, seeing the rain bashing the brown tiles of the roof below me, bouncing about in a torrent of silver before draining away into the gutter. I couldn't use the steps down, they'd see me and then who knew what would happen. So instead, I came to the edge of the retaining wall where I could see the felt roof of the shed, right below me. I got down on my hands and knees, eased myself around, and lowered myself down the wall on to the roof of the shed. I was already soaked and muddy, so didn't care too much how filthy I became with my body pressed up against the mossy, dripping wall. My feet found the gritty felt of the shed roof and I allowed it to take my weight. I was sure it would hold.

How wrong I was.

I took two steps towards the front of the shed and the whole thing gave way beneath me.

30.

I landed on the table where Joanne potted vegetables in the spring.

Thankfully it didn't break, which meant I didn't fall too far or onto anything nasty like the lawn mower or the garden spade and fork, which were propped up against the wall.

But I landed hard on my butt and it hurt so bad I started to cry.

And then heard a shout outside and realised those two must have heard me.

'No!' I was so angry and frightened I shouted out loud. It felt like an invisible hand had grabbed me by the throat. Even though it hurt like hell I pushed myself off the table and unlatched the door in front of me.

Amid the din of the rain I heard the hinges of the front gate squeal. They were coming in!

There was nowhere for me to hide. I could squeeze myself in between the retaining wall that ran back around the kitchen but they would surely find me and then I'd be completely trapped. My only hope was to try to reach the back door.

I regretted the decision as soon as I came around the corner of the house and saw the two men running up the garden, the Wookiee in the lead.

'What do you want?' I shrieked. I didn't notice the back door, just a couple of metres away from me, opening.

'What do you think you're up to?'

Suddenly Grandpa Bob was there, in between me and the men. Bizarrely, he was in his old white towel dressing gown, faded to yellowish beige on the shoulders and collar. He liked his afternoon bath and I guessed he must have been in the kitchen making himself a cup of tea to take up for the long soak.

The men stopped in front of Grandpa Bob, incongruous with his messy grey hair and skinny legs, standing there in the downpour.

'You tell him,' said the Wookiee, pointing at me over Grandpa Bob's shoulder, 'to leave him alone.'

'What?' said Grandpa Bob.

'Tell him to leave him alone,' said the other man, in a thin, reedy voice. He was tall, slightly stooped. He looked like some kind of intellectual, a university professor or something.

'What on earth are you talking about?' said Grandpa Bob. He glanced back at me. I was rubbing my butt. 'Get inside, Daniel,' he said, then added quickly: 'Are you all right?'

I nodded, throwing the briefest glance at the scary, hostile face of the Wookiee before darting around Grandpa Bob into the house.

'Now you two, I don't know who the hell you are, but you'd both better bugger off out of our garden right now or I'm calling the police,' he said.

'You tell that kid to leave him alone,' said the Wookiee once again. I was standing at the threshold, out of sight, holding on to the edge of the door and listening.

'Who are you talking about?' said Grandpa Bob.

'The man in the woods. Tell him to keep away from him. For good. Or there'll be trouble.'

'I…' Grandpa Bob actually chuckled. 'I really don't know who you mean, or what you're talking about. I think you are both most likely stark raving mad. But if you don't skedaddle right this minute, you're going to be the ones in trouble. Two grown men threatening a child? I don't know what's got into you!'

There was a moment of silence – well, except for the rain – when I imagined them all eyeballing one another. And then another squeak of the gate, followed by the clatter of bikes being lifted and prepared. And then Grandpa Bob came back into the house, soaked through in his dressing gown, his hair all stuck around the top of his head.

He let out a deep sigh and said: 'Tell me what's going on, Daniel.'

31

Sitting at the kitchen table, whilst Grandpa Bob towel dried his hair, I told him about the man in the woods.

I told him how I'd first come across him out there, making his den, and how I'd recognised him off the telly. I told him how I'd taken him chips but he didn't seem to want them as he was fasting. I didn't go into all the details of the other times I'd seen him, but I did tell him that the man appeared to be a bit sick today.

'Daniel,' said Grandpa Bob, sipping his tea, 'I don't have to tell you that you should never speak to strange men. What would your mother say?'

I shrugged, wondering where she even was. Must be upstairs with Sally. With all that nursing and being up in the night, she'd probably fallen asleep. Slept right through the encounter with the Wookiee and his professor pal.

'And now these other two oafs have appeared, we're going to have to refer it all to the police. We can't have them coming back looking for you. God knows what they're up to, it could be some kind of criminal gang or something. Maybe something to do with drugs.'

I thought for a moment then said: 'I guess you're right, Grandpa. Although…'

'What?'

'I don't know. There's something about that man. He doesn't like talking about his challenge. At first I wondered if he was doing one of those televised things, you know, like Bear Grylls, living out in the wilderness with nothing to help him except his bare hands and a knife. You know the sort of thing. But there's no cameras or anything. And I kind of respect him for that. I don't know what the police will do if they find him, but they could spoil it for him.'

And spoil it for me, too, I thought. I wasn't sure how but felt it in my bones. If the police were involved, anything could happen.

'I don't really care what they spoil for him,' said Grandpa Bob. 'I'm not having you being threatened.'

'Look, I'll just stay away from him,' I said after a pause. 'I don't know why they care, they're probably worried that I'll upset their game or something. But if it means so much to them I won't go back and see him.'

Grandpa Bob looked at me. I stared at his narrow jaw and mouth, the rough grey stubble, then said: 'Please don't call the police, Grandpa.'

His eyes closed slightly, like a cornered cat.

32.

I struggled in school the next day.

The rain was so relentless it gave an oppressive gloom even to the indoors. The teachers turned on the lights but school fluorescent strips have the knack of making things feel somehow even more miserable. Johnny didn't even meet my eye when I sauntered past his desk on the way to my own. Gemma did, though, and I noticed a flash of something triumphant there before she quickly looked back down at her reading book, her cheeks flushing pink.

It was one of my worst days, full of maths and science, and my mind wouldn't stop wandering. I thought about the man, sick in the rain in the woods, and wondered how he would cope. Was it possible to die like that, from hypothermia or something? I thought too about the Wookiee and his mate, what they were up to, and would they do much more of it? I thought about Sally and her injury and Grandpa Bob and what he was going to do. I could see so much, so many routes and possibilities, and it had the effect of almost shutting me down completely. It was all so utterly… portentous.

That was the word, wasn't it? Miss Hailey used it last term, teaching us about the Ancient Greeks and their omens. I'd had to look it up.

Yes, portentous. That's what it was.

To say the least.

33.

When I got home guess who was coming out the garden gate as I slowed down on my bike?

The social workers, May and Paul. The house was becoming like Piccadilly Circus.

'Hello, Daniel,' said Paul, unlatching the gate. 'We've been with your mum and grandad, looking at the film of Sally.'

'Oh,' I said.

'It looks like she might have managed to hurt herself,' he said.

He walked up close to me, May beside him. She reached out and touched my hand. 'We're going to keep an eye on things,' she said. 'But we wanted you to know that we really care about you, Daniel.'

I remembered to smile.

'Yes, we do,' said Paul. He took off his spectacles and wiped his left eye with the sleeve of his corduroy jacket.

'You can – you must – contact us if anything more untoward happens,' said May. The touch turned into a light grip on my fingers. 'Anything,' she stressed and looked me hard in the eye. There was so much feeling in there. I just couldn't tell what type.

'You're a very special child,' she said.

'Yes,' said Paul, and wiped his other eye. Then he put his glasses back on. 'Your grandad mentioned some strange men. We can protect you…'

'We love you, Daniel,' May interrupted.

I pulled my hand away from her and pushed my bike past them into the gate.

'We love you, Daniel!' Paul repeated. He was quite solemn.

I didn't look back.

Grown-ups. They can love you even when you didn't try.

Especially when you didn't try.

34.

I let myself in with my key.

The kitchen was deserted but two teabags bobbed in a couple of mugs of steaming water. I went through the dining room and hall and found Grandpa Bob and Joanne in the front room. Grandpa Bob was playing with Sally on the floor and Joanne was sitting on the leather sofa, watching.

'You're going to be trouble aren't you, little miss?' said Grandpa Bob, holding her tiny wrists and moving them left to right as Sally cooed on her back by the fire grate. There was no protection for the little fire, the grate just protruded out over the carpet. Despite the chill weather, they hadn't lit it.

'Did you see the social workers, Daniel?' Joanne asked as I slumped down on one of the armchairs.

'Yes.'

'They watched Grandpa's films,' she said. 'They think she broke her leg on her own.'

I looked at the bandage, still wrapped around Sally's lower leg. The splint had been gone a long time now.

'That's good,' I said.

'Trouble for your ma and pa,' Grandpa Bob continued, moving his big face closer to the baby. She watched him steadily. I thought she looked like she couldn't quite believe him, that he was there.

'It's a bloody relief,' said Joanne. She glanced at the onyx box on the coffee table, the one with the cigarettes.

'A weight off all our minds,' said Grandpa Bob, without looking up.

I looked out the window. The rain had stopped after lunch but the afternoon gloom hadn't gone away. I saw the tops of the nearby trees, raking the grey clouds with their black branches. What was he doing now?

'I found that man today,' said Grandpa Bob, easing himself up on to his knees and swivelling to glance at me.

'What?'

'The man you told me about,' said Grandpa Bob.

'How?' I asked.

'Just on my walk,' he said.

I felt my skin shrinking around my ears and forehead. Of course he could find him. Grandpa Bob and I had walked all my favourite routes over the years. Why hadn't I thought of that?

'How was he? Still ill?' I asked.

'What man is that?' said Joanne.

'Urr,' said the baby.

'Some kind of homeless chap,' said Grandpa Bob. 'He's not the one you think he is, Daniel, I'm sure. He's not that guy off the telly.'

'What guy off the telly?' said Joanne.

'Nothing,' I said.

'Daniel has found a man who's sleeping rough in the woods,' said Grandpa Bob, looking at his daughter. 'He's been out there for a few weeks. Daniel thought he was someone off the TV, one of those war protestors outside parliament, but I'm sure he's not. Looks a bit like him, but he's not.'

'He is,' I said, then added: 'Is he still sick?'

'He said he's had a bit of a fever, but he's over the worst now.'

'Did he say why he was staying out there? Is it some kind of challenge?' I said.

'No, he didn't seem to want to talk about it,' said Grandpa Bob. 'But he did tell me about the dog.'

'What?'

'The one you took back to its owner. The injured one.'

'Oh, Toby,' I said.

'Mr Jackson's dog?' said Joanne.

'Yes,' I said.

'You're a good boy, Daniel,' said Grandpa Bob. 'He seems a fairly harmless one to me. But don't go visiting him again, will you?'

35.

A terrible shriek broke the silence of the house that night.

'Daniel!' shouted Richard as he met me on the landing, dimly lit by the small red light of the smoke alarm above our heads. 'Are you all right?'

'Yes,' I said, pushing open Sally's door. 'The baby…' I added.

We both went in, Richard flicking on the main light.

The baby was thrashing around in her cot, wailing. He reached in then stopped, checking for injuries. He was barged out of the way by Joanne who arrived, lifting the baby and hugging her close to her chest. Joanne was making a strange grunting noise.

'I didn't want to lift her in case she'd broken something else,' said Richard. He was tall and spindly and white in his black boxer shorts. His hair fanned out at the back like a seventies rock star, the result of a ponytail you only undid at night.

Joanne ignored him, staring closely into the baby's face. She at least was wearing a T-shirt that hung down over the tops of her large thighs.

Outside I could hear Grandpa Bob's door open.

'What is it?' he called. His voice was hoarse.

I backed off as he came into the cot room. They were all looking at the baby, saying urgent things, and I found it too much. Overloading. The baby was OK, I reckoned she wouldn't be shrieking that much if she was seriously hurt. I decided to retreat silently back to my room.

I was unnoticed by the grown-ups.

36.

'Bloody thing!'

With all the wailing and shouting and knocking about upstairs I couldn't sleep, so I went downstairs to get a glass of milk.

Grandpa Bob had made the exclamation. He was in the kitchen in his dressing gown, trying to connect a lead from the camera to the laptop. I yawned.

'What's wrong with it?' I asked.

'The screen's on the blink,' he said. 'I'm trying a different cable.'

I yawned again and opened the fridge. The faint smell of mould wafted out and I could see Richard had put a half-sliced onion in there, without peeling off its brown skin. I wrinkled my nose and reached in for the milk.

'Blast!' Things were not going well for Grandpa Bob.

I poured my milk and walked over to the seat. I swung my leg over the bench and sat down beside him. He was fretting, I could see, his swollen knuckles were pale and shaking as he finally connected the small plug. He was an old man, after all, and it was the middle of the night. He shouldn't have to put up with all this.

'Let's try this one…' he said.

I yawned again – couldn't stop, really – and watched as the image from the night camera came on the screen.

There she was, little Sally, lifting her arms up over her head and then… the whiteness imploded in on itself, losing her, then there were lines flicking up and down, black and white, all the mayhem of corrupt technology and then… blackness. Or greyness, to be more accurate.

Grandpa Bob swore properly then, using the f-bomb.

'Why do you think it isn't working?' I said.

'I've no idea, Daniel,' he said sharply.

I decided to keep quiet.

'Sorry,' he said. 'I don't know. It was fine the day before yesterday.'

He played it from the start again. The baby's arms went up, the screen imploded, lines appeared, then nothing.

'Not working, is it,' I said.

'To say the bloody ob…' he said, before stopping himself. 'Let me play it one more time…'

He pushed the keys and it replayed. Just as the baby lifted her arms this time he clicked the screen to pause it.

Grandpa Bob leaned in and scrutinised the image with his bloodshot, rheumy eyes. I sipped my milk.

'What's that there?'

'Where?' I said, leaning forward. The baby wailed from somewhere upstairs and for a moment I thought it was on the screen. Then remembered there was no sound.

Grandpa Bob pointed at the bottom right-hand corner. I frowned.

'Can you see that?' he said.

I shrugged. 'What?'

He traced the outline of something. It looked like a lump of black, curved at the end.

'Isn't it just where it's about to mess up?' I said.

'I don't know,' he said and hit the key to restart the film. In the next moment, the screen fractured and went dead again.

I tipped the remainder of the milk down my throat and stood up as he hit the back arrow. He was still watching the short clip on repeat when I set my glass in the sink and headed back upstairs.

37.

It was a terrible night and I thought I would never get to sleep. The baby was making a sound like nothing on earth, like the shriek train wheels make against rails, like the sound monkeys make when they're battling in the jungle at night, like… I don't know.

Like the sound a baby makes, when things have got very bad for it.

I was lying in my bed, watching the glow-in-the-dark stars that had been stuck on my ceiling since I was small, wondering if she would ever stop screaming, if Richard and Joanne were going to take her to hospital, if Grandpa Bob would come to any conclusions about the film, if the man in the woods would…

I woke up at 6.32am according to my digital clock.

There was a grey luminosity around my curtains, a little light coming in from outside because the clocks had gone forward a week or two ago. I realised that despite the noise I must have dropped off for an hour or two. I was tired and didn't want to think about it all again but…

I knew I had to.

I had to make some decisions. Things were important. They couldn't be more so.

It was Tuesday, a school day, but I knew if I was quick I had time. I got dressed in my jeans and sweatshirt then went downstairs. The house was deathly quiet, I enjoyed the hush of it.

In the kitchen I had another glass of milk then put on my trainers, picked up my keys, and went out through the backdoor.

Moments later, I collected my bike from the shed with its temporary polythene roof, which had been fitted and tacked into place by Grandpa Bob. I wheeled the bike down the garden and out of the gate, then cycled to the point where the road gives way to the bark-mulchy track.

Then I was up and away into the fresh cool scent of it all, amid the din of a thousand birds sounding their dismal dawn cacophony.

Why did we have to share the world with all these crazy creatures, I wondered, squabbling for their tiny slice of territory each day?

What a set up…

38.

Skellig, the book, was in my head again as I reached the clearing where he'd set himself up these last few weeks.

The bird-angel thing. The guardian angel. Would he rise to the occasion?

He was asleep again, damp, underneath his makeshift roof of whips, beside the black wet ash of last night's fire. His hair was splayed across brown and ruddy-copper leaves, tangled with small twigs. The hygiene issues, I thought. As I approached him there was a low knocking sound above and I jumped. Then realised it was just another one of those restless birds, a woodpecker, thumping its head into the tree above me.

'Hello.'

His eyes opened and were quickly on me. He sat up, drawing in a deep breath through his narrow nostrils.

He rubbed the back of his head with his hand. His slowness implied stiffness in his muscles and joints.

'Are you feeling better?' I asked.

He nodded slowly, closed his eyes. Then sighed and looked back up at me. He remained sitting on the ground, knees akimbo.

I smiled at him, in what I thought was a knowing manner. 'You're a healer, aren't you?' I said.

He looked at me.

'I know you must be. The way you found that dog, Mr Jackson's dog, Toby, and patched up its wound. The way you care about society and war and stuff. You're a healer.'

'Where are you going with this?' he asked. He didn't sound enthusiastic.

'Why didn't you heal yourself if you're a healer?' I asked. 'When you got sick the other day.'

'I'm not a healer,' he said.

'But you are, you helped the dog. And I need a healer. Not me, I'm OK – kind of – but for my sister. My baby sister. She's hurt, you see. I told you about her broken leg which we thought was because she was shifting around too much in her cot and we thought she must have got it stuck between the slats because Grandpa Bob put a camera up so we saw how much she moved which was good because social services had got involved and we were worried they might take her away but the camera proved it was just her but then last night in the middle of the night she started wailing again, really shrieking, it was the worst sound you ever heard, just coming from this tiny little baby, this poor little thing…'

'Stop.'

'What?'

'You heard.'

I was astonished. He didn't cease to astonish me.

'If you could just come and help her? Help her with your healing. I know you could…'

'Go.'

'A tiny little thing, she is. So sweet… and vulnerable. If you could just come once, just a quick visit, you might…'

'Go away.'

I put my palm on my forehead, pushed up my fringe.

'You don't care about a baby?' I said.

'I'm not coming, I'm sorry. We've talked about this before. It's my challenge, I need to be here for a certain time and I can't break it.'

'How long?'

'No is the answer.'

'She's…'

I looked at his face. He was staring off into the morning forest. It was brightening with the dawn, silvery light filtering through the bars of the tree trunks. It was like a release from prison. The birds were crying out in the air, all because of the arrival of the light.

I... I...

39.

I headed home.

I saw a snail on the path and rode over it, smashing its shell to a pulp.

I screamed at the forest.

I swerved my handlebars too fast, willing myself to crash and get hurt. Somehow I stayed upright.

I screamed again.

As I came within earshot of the house, I stopped and sucked in deep breaths, knowing I had to control myself. The anger didn't assuage, it was a red-hot poker striking me inside, every bit of me was lashing out from the hurt. I was a pit of vipers, surprised by a dumb beast, biting chaotically. I didn't know how I would be, back in the company of my family.

As I was standing there with my bike between my legs I heard something. Talking. Men talking. Coming towards me. I realised I should get out of the way, hide, but then they appeared ahead of me, coming round a bend on the path.

Too late, I recognised them.

It was Grandpa Bob, going for his early morning walk. Grandpa Bob, speaking to another old man, though not as old as him.

A man in a flat cap and grey moleskin jacket. A man it took me a moment or two to recognise. But when I did I felt a sudden shift of gravity.

It was Mr Jackson.

I couldn't cope with this. In plain sight of them, perhaps just twenty metres away, I dropped my bike and ran off into the trees.

I heard Grandpa Bob shout my name as I disappeared.

40.

My head was a storm of confusion.

I didn't know where to go, what to do. I had to be at school. I'd left my bike behind, there on the path. I needed it to get to school. What would Grandpa Bob do, would he pick it up and bring it home? What was he saying to Mr Jackson?

Why wouldn't the man come and save my baby sister?

I was sure Skellig would have.

After roaming through the woods for an unknown period, cursing the chirping of the birds, the scratching of squirrels on bark, and everything I knew, I found myself at the foot of the incline that led up to the folly. I decided to make my way up there, to get a view on things, the helicopter view, they called it, didn't they? It was all I could think to do. I had probably missed registration by now, anyway.

It was a good call. The view from the top was what I needed, down, down across the serried forest to the open fields, the long, flat earth. Big sky, grey sky. An emptiness to hold my mind. It was so rarely empty.

I breathed in the air through my nostrils, felt my lungs expand, pushed out my chest. I was crying, I could feel the tears on my cheeks. There was so much, so much in the world, so much… demanded of me.

What was I going to do? I knew I needed to act fast now, there was so little time left but…

What should I do?

41

When I got home he was there, in the garden, bending over, planting bulbs with a trowel.

Grandpa Bob. In his black felt hat.

He stood up straight, nearly straight, holding on to his back, when he heard me open the gate. He looked at me as I stepped into the garden. I glanced away, saw my bike propped against the shed.

'You're missing school,' he said.

When I didn't reply, he went on: 'Why did you run away, Daniel?'

I started to walk past him, towards my bike.

'I'll go now, just say I overslept,' I said.

He put his hand on my shoulder to stop me.

'What happened with Mr Jackson's dog?' he said.

I screwed my eyes shut.

'Daniel?'

'He ran away!' I blurted. 'He ran away and I felt so bad I'd lost him that I didn't tell him!'

A beat. Then I looked up at his old face, the narrow jaw with the deep black creases from lips to nose. His brown eyes watching me carefully.

'You should have told me or your parents,' he said. 'We would have told him for you.'

'I was scared,' I said. Then added: 'Scared of you all being cross with me. That's all you ever do, you're all either ignoring me or else you're angry with me. All everyone does is think about *her* all the time!'

'That's not true, Daniel,' he said. 'We all love you very much.'

'It's how I feel!'

He put an arm around my shoulder and squeezed me against him, a bony shoulder-to-ribcage hug.

'Come in, I'll make you a cup of tea,' he said.

'No – no, I'll go to school,' I said.

'Are you sure? You don't have to. I know things have been tough for you recently. No one will begrudge you a day off. A duvet day.'

'I'm sure,' I said quietly, then marched over to collect my bike. As I pushed it back past him towards the gate I noticed the look on his face. It was strange. I've told you how I can't read expressions well, but even I could see the odd things going on there. Grandpa Bob was worried, there was no doubt about that. But I could tell there was something else there, something that made me worried. Or at least, more worried than I was already. Which was super, ultra-worried.

'Ride carefully,' he said, as I pushed off down the road.

I glanced back once and saw him standing there, still and watching. His mouth was open a little. Agape.

My reading of faces might not be good, but my instincts were.

Something had changed.

42.

I put up my hand.

'Sitting in a different spot, today, Mr Page?'

'Yes, Miss.' I smiled at Miss Hailey and threw a quick glance sideways. Johnny was beside me, squirming. He'd been sitting alone and I hadn't given him a choice. Stuff that Gemma Tees.

'Go on, then, tell us – what do Christians believe will happen at the end of time?'

'There will be the final judgement, Miss,' I said. 'Jesus will come again and sort the righteous from the wicked.'

'Exactly. So what happens to people when they die?'

I kind of knew but didn't want to seem like I was bragging so kept silent. I looked at Johnny to see if he had any idea. He looked gormless and baffled and I wondered why I had ever bothered with him.

'There is the particular judgement,' Miss Hailey said to the quiet class. 'It's an intermediate judgement, at which point people's souls either go to Heaven, to Hell, or to Purgatory.'

'Or to Load of Old Baloney,' said Michael Devon. Everyone, even little Tommy Locks who took his study so seriously, laughed. Michael had clearly meant to say it under his breath, but his voice was breaking and it came out deep.

Miss Hailey stared at him. She was a nice teacher and could get everyone focused but she didn't rule the roost, she wasn't powerful enough. I thought she was going to lose control, everyone was going to go wild. But somehow, her poise, that niceness and calmness, held sway and people quietened down.

'Can someone remind us what Purgatory is?' she said.

'It's a place where people who have done some wrong things go, when they haven't done enough of them to go to Hell,' I heard Gemma say behind me. 'Once they've done their time there, they get to go to Heaven.'

I looked back over my shoulder at her. She saw and watched me for a moment. Her face took on a strange aspect.

'Turn around, Daniel,' said Miss Hailey.

'Yes, Miss.'

I did, in the process giving Johnny a big smile.

Gormless, definitely. Why had I ever bothered?

43

Joanne was in the kitchen when I got home.

'All right, Daniel?' she said, as I came in.

'Yes, thanks,' I said. 'Where is everyone?'

She was down on her knees on the tile floor, shoving sick-stained blankets and baby suits into the washing machine.

'Sally's asleep in her cot,' she said. 'And your grandpa is having his bath.'

Richard of course was still at work. For a moment, I wondered about him sitting there at his desk with his computer in an office full of workers. Wondered whether he was ever tempted to try it on again. Fraud. Stealing from his company. Did he have the guts or had he learnt his lesson now? Whoever knew the workings of the human soul…

I went and stood beside Joanne. She ignored me and carried on feeding the laundry into the drum. I noticed the waft of the sour, milky sick and wrinkled my nose. I also noticed the pale grey bruises on her forearms as her sweatshirt sleeves drew back each time she thrust her arms into the machine.

'How did you get those?' I asked.

'What?'

'The bruises.'

She didn't even look up. 'Just the baby gripping. You know how easily I bruise. My skin's thin as paper.'

I stood there looking down at her.

'Are you hungry, Daniel?' she asked, shutting the machine door. She stood up. 'There's some hot cross buns in the bread bin if you need a snack.'

'No, I'm all right,' I said.

'I'm making chicken pie for later,' she said. 'Ready about half six.'

I nodded and picked up my bag and carried it upstairs.

I paused for a moment, hearing a light splashing coming from the bathroom at the end of the landing. Grandpa Bob was humming quietly to himself in the bath. There was no sound from the baby's room, but the door was ajar. I could see the room was darkened by the curtains being drawn.

I went in.

Now the clocks had gone forward it was still daylight outside, so I could see the room clearly despite the curtains. There was the chest of drawers by the cot with the pink bedside light, over which Joanne had draped a flimsy scarf to soften its glare when it was on. There was the rainbow fish and bubble stickers I'd helped Richard put on the wall. There was the mosaic of small, fluffy whales, seals and dolphins suspended between the cot and the window. A toy rabbit slanting over on the chair, and a few picture books scattered on the floor. And the camera above the cot, reinstated after the baby's distress the night before.

And there, in the bed, sound asleep, was Sally.

I stood and looked at her, in her blue bodysuit, arms neatly pinning down by her covering blanket. Her head was turned to her right, the non-existent jaw tipped up slightly, presumably to aid her breathing, which I could hear if I listened carefully now Grandpa Bob's humming had stopped. Her eyebrows were raised as if she was questioning something. I smelt the faint whiff of milk-sick I'd noticed in the kitchen, and thought about the struggles the body had to make itself function better over time.

Clever, it was all so clever. But to what end? Babies were born, children grew, adults stagnated, old people died. That was it, wasn't it? Boil it all down, that was the game. Choices made no difference in the end.

Or did they?

'Daniel!'

I realised I had leaned in over her and froze when I heard Grandpa Bob's voice behind me.

I turned and saw him standing in the doorway in his dressing gown, his thin grey hair still damp around the top of his head. I could see beads of water or possibly sweat on the mottled skin of his brow.

'What are you doing? She's asleep,' he said.

'I just wanted to look at her,' I said. 'She's so sweet.'

I frowned then because, even in the muted light, I could tell he didn't believe me.

44.

Later, I cycled hard through the grey forest.

The speed brought my senses up and I could hear every twitch in the undergrowth, see the spider that spun its web from a branch, feel the oxygen-rich air sieving through my alveoli. Or at least, it felt like I could.

I was determined to give him one last chance.

The man in the woods.

One last chance.

45.

Darkness was seeping through the trees and bracken as I approached his camp.

I saw the fire laid out, his tatty old bed mat under the shelter and a metal water bottle. His canvas backpack, surely mildewed by now with all the rain.

But he wasn't there.

'Hello!' I said, not quite as loudly as I'd planned. Was I scared?

No answer.

I crept forward and prodded the kindling with the tip of my trainer. There was a pen knife lying in the mud, the small blade halfway out.

I turned to look at his pack and shrieked as a hand landed heavily on my shoulder.

'What do you want?'

He had appeared out of nowhere and was looking down at me with those eyes, fierce and disturbing, a little too close together.

'I… I've come to ask you again,' I said, drawing away from his grasp. 'Will you come and help her?'

'Your sister?'

'Yes.'

'No.'

'She's ill, she's small, you're this great activist and healer, why not?'

'You know why not.'

'I don't!' I said. But I did, of course. I always had.

He turned away towards the laid fire.

'Please,' I added.

He knelt and fished in his pocket, brought out some matches.

'You're not going to come, are you?' I said.

His soil-stained fingers eased open the box and he picked out a match.

'You don't really care, do you?' I said.

He struck the match and in the gloom I saw his features sharpen with contrast, the bright forehead and nose and dark mouth, shadowed eyes. He almost looked like one of us.

'She needs someone to save her,' I said.

He held the match to the smaller wood at the base of the fire.

'I'll give you all this,' I said.

He didn't even look up as I gestured behind and around me. Just continued to watch as the match flame claimed the smaller twigs for its own, whilst all the time working towards his stained fingers. He must have kept those twigs dry somehow, I thought, and wondered how he'd done it.

'The woods, fields, they're all yours if you want them. The town…'

His mouth twitched at the edges.

'No argument,' I said. 'It's all yours. Just come and help my sister.'

'Bugger off,' he said.

46.

I went home in tears.

He didn't care, did he, not one little bit? He didn't give a shit. I would show him…

It was almost completely dark by the time I neared our house on the edge of the woods. I didn't have my lights but luckily I knew the way like the back of my hand, knew all the kinks in the path and the small stones and roots and pits that could send you flying if you took them wrong.

As I came down the track that met our road I saw lights flashing through the trees. Blue lights.

I reached forward and grabbed my brakes, slowed the bike as it rattled down the slope. Took the turn on to the broader track, then came on to the tarmac outside the house.

The road was entirely blocked by an ambulance. There was a thump and then a man in green came round from the back and opened the cabin door. He climbed in, without noticing me. I watched as he leaned forward and started the engine.

'Daniel!'

The ambulance was such a spectacle I hadn't noticed Richard and Joanne standing in the garden near the gate, watching. It was Richard who had spotted me.

The ambulance began to reverse, its lights turning our house and the bushes opposite into a silent, lacklustre disco. Its going made it easier for me to wheel my bike up to them. I saw the tears in Joanne's eyes.

'What's happened?' I said.

'It's your grandpa,' said Richard. 'He's had a stroke.'

47.

I stayed in the kitchen with them for as long as I could bear it.

They were both drinking alcohol, Richard a red wine and Joanne a craft beer, worrying about Grandpa Bob.

'Are you OK?' Joanne asked me at one stage.

I grimaced and gave a small nod.

'I'm going to go to the hospital and wait,' Joanne said as she pushed her half-drunk bottle away across the table.

'They told us not to right now, said it was best to wait,' said Richard. 'They'll call if there's any change in his condition.'

'He's my dad,' said Joanne.

'What about the baby?'

'She fed less than an hour ago and there's a bottle in the fridge.'

'OK.' Richard grimaced too. We all knew he wasn't good with the baby. 'We could all go,' he said, after a moment.

'There's no point,' said Joanne. 'They don't know how long he will be out. I'll come back if Sally needs me.'

I'd gathered that Grandpa Bob had been unconscious when they found him. He hadn't regained consciousness all the time it took for the ambulance to arrive and take him away. It made me wonder how they knew it was a stroke but I didn't want to ask.

'Look, get me a water bottle and some fruit and a cereal bar,' she said, standing up. 'I'll go now.'

'OK,' said Richard, which was when I sidled off upstairs.

48.

I sat in my room staring at half-painted dark elves under my desk lamp and listening to rain swish against the window.

I heard the bang of the back door as Joanne left, followed by the squeal of the gate, the blip of the car lock, the clunk of a door and start of a motor. She drove off.

Downstairs, Richard went into the lounge and turned on the television. I heard TV laughter reverberate through the walls and floorboards before he turned it down. Grandpa Bob had been watching in the afternoon, he always turned it up too loud.

I sighed, and looked at my reflection in the blackness of the window. I stared at my eyes, saw them glow in the pale light.

Show them to Grandpa Bob. That was all I'd needed to do when he found me with the baby the second time, and realised it was me who'd switched off the camera before. Maybe guessed the truth about the dog, then, too.

Show him my eyes.

Show him my real eyes, full of the fire of home.

It was no good, I thought. The man wasn't coming, was he? I'd done everything I could, offered him my kingdom, the woods, suggested we jump from the tower, tried to give him chips but…

It just wasn't happening.

Even my new idea, come to save the baby, had failed. The poor little baby.

I could feel myself losing control, feel the shockwaves of despair, of powerlessness and eternal torment blasting through me like the raggedy old world itself. I put my head on my arm and stayed like that, staring wide eyed at the grain of wood on my desk, the black cuts in the burnished wood.

I stayed like that for a while, thinking I should leave it all there, just… give up.

I went into a kind of torpor.

I don't how long for.

Staring.

At the desk.

Battered and bereft.

The desk.

Me.

Staring at the black grain of the wood in front of my eyes, a little yellowish, almost gold in places, reflecting the light from the lamp.

What to do?

What?

49.

My anger is my superpower.

It struck me like a whip behind the eyes.

I sat bolt upright, caught another glimpse of my eyes, bright and burning, reflected in the black window.

I would not give up.

He would not get the better of me this time. Not again. Who did he think I was?

I stood up, hearing a clatter behind me as my chair tipped back and struck the floorboards. I looked at my desk and saw the small scalpel I used to cut my model pieces from their runners. I snatched it up and went out of my room and into the baby's.

I turned on the light and marched up to the cot.

Sally was in there sleeping, just like earlier. The little fingers of her right hand were moving ever so slightly at the corner of her mouth. There was a small kink above her eye, the starting of a frown. This was it, the paragon of creation, dribbling its goo.

I realised then that his coming here, coming here to *my woods*, was no accident. No, he'd come because he knew I was here too. It had been necessary for him, necessary somehow in the grand, the oh-so-bloody-grand, scheme of things.

The temptation.

And all I had tried had failed. I had done everything in my power. The same – or at least similar – three temptations as last time, the food, the test of faith by leaping off the folly, the offer of my whole world, the woods and the town – plus this new one I'd come up with, which I thought was best of all. How could he resist it, saving a poor, tiny baby, the greatest of all beings, filled with all that promise and potential?

Clearly, he could.

On that first day, I'd pitched myself from my bike to injure myself and later crept in and hurt her in the night, knowing I had to make as a big a commotion as possible to have any chance of him finding out, out there in the wilderness. And the best way to do that, as I knew so well, was to involve Institutions. Human Institutions! They can't help but make a mess of things. Those social workers... they had liked me, *adored* me even, I hadn't expected that, but then again I do have a certain special charm – they had got involved and then, almost certainly because of them, the Wookiee, who was probably one of the man's followers, *disciples*, whatever you call them – and the professor too, and they must have had means of getting word to the man, of confirming all the things I said were true.

But what I still couldn't work out was why he had to do the whole forty days and nights in the wilderness thing again. There just didn't seem to be any point the second time round. I had really stewed on that one. Then realised I could think about it all eternity – or I could just accept it and move on.

Yes, it had been a good plan. Force him out to save the baby. But...

It hadn't worked.

So now there was only one thing left to do, to make him break his vow and get him out of the woods.

The option I was never keen on, because it was so unsubtle.

The nuclear option, you could call it.

I reached into the cot, pushed down the blanket, and exposed the baby's chest in its bodysuit, its tiny bare neck. It murmured, fidgeted with its collar, but remained asleep.

I raised the scalpel, preparing to strike.

And a blinding light filled the room.

50.

I stumbled backwards, covering my eyes with my forearm and dropping the scalpel.

The curtains, the windows themselves, were no longer there, in fact half the side of the house seemed to have vanished. In their place was… well, what can I say?

In their place was him.

The man from the woods.

Except now he was larger, and he was floating in the air, and he had brought the sun, his sun, with him.

Light flashed around him, not the cold blue flashing light of an ambulance, but the superpower light of the stuff that underpins reality. It was a light mixed with Malakim and Erelim and Seraphim and all the rest of them, whirling around with their silver wings and gold trumpets and their heads held high with oh-so-righteous anger.

There were sheep and horned cows and doves and exquisite books. There were incandescent stars pricking at a sumptuous purple firmament.

Yes, it was all there. Just as those visionary medieval illustrators would have it.

And all of it surrounding him, the man, with his wind-whipped hair and beard and his open palms and changed-into-white robes and – above all – with his eyes, his eyes of pulsing fire and judgement, his eyes of anger and justice, his eyes of blue and…

Sadness. His eyes of vast, human, sadness.

All there, before me, outside our little house on the edge of the dark wood.

Our little house on the edge of the dark wood.

It bears repeating: our little house *on the edge* of the dark wood.

The man had left the woods. *He had left his wilderness.*

As I cowered from the blinding light, I felt a million tiny horned ones dancing with joy in my belly.

After what felt like several minutes of the light show – I wondered briefly how Richard in the living room was experiencing all this – I saw the intensity drop.

Then he spoke. It was a voice like his own but through a boom box. It set my teeth on edge.

'Go.'

That was it.

'But,' I replied, 'it's only thirty-seven days – by my reckoning.'

There was no reply.

The lights stopped and I looked back round.

The man was gone.

I went, of course.

I left because I had to, faced with a superior force.

I left the screaming baby, I didn't reply to Richard as he yelled at me, barging past as he came up the stairs and I went down. In the hallway, I heard the television, it was the news.

'…three people shot in the embassy before special forces stormed the building and killed the hostage takers… the Prime Minister is convening an emergency Cobra meeting of ministers and senior Armed Forces personnel tonight…'

I went to the front door, turned the latch, and stepped outside.

I breathed in the cool air, felt rain splash on my raised cheeks.

My final ploy *had* worked. I had banked on the idea that, for him, it was never just a numbers game. It was always about the individual. It's what set him apart from so many others. Maybe even his Dad. Sure, there were plenty of kids suffering in the world – *plenty* – but when one of those was right there, in front of his nose…

Well, he couldn't help himself.

And that, of course, was his weak spot.

53.

I left because I had to, faced with a superior force.

But I left with a smile, because the larger victory was mine. In fact, let's face it, I had won. He had left the woods before his time was up, three days short of his forty. He'd broken his vow to himself.

He had revealed his power – and his vulnerability.

I opened the garden gate, thought about taking a left into the woods or a right into town, into civilisation.

I turned right.

Things are going to be different from now on.

THE END

Thank you for reading my book, I hope you enjoyed it!

If you did, I would be very grateful if you could post a rating or short review on Amazon or Goodreads. Your ratings make a real difference to authors, helping the books you enjoy reach more people.

Other Books by Steve Griffin

The Ghosts of Alice

The Ghosts of Alice is a series of standalone ghost stories featuring Alice Deaton, a young woman with a mysterious connection to the dead.

The Boy in the Burgundy Hood

** THE #1 INTERNATIONAL BESTSELLER **

Will it be her dream job – or a waking nightmare?

Alice can't believe her luck when she lands a new post at a medieval English manor house. Mired in debt, the elderly owners have transferred their beloved Bramley to a heritage trust. Alice must prepare it for opening to the public, with the former owners relegated to a private wing.

But when the ghosts start appearing – the woman with the wounded hand and the boy in the burgundy hood – Alice realises why her predecessor might have left the isolated house so soon.

As she peels back the layers of the mystery, the secrets Alice uncovers haunting Bramley's heart will be dark – darker than she could ever have imagined…

What readers say about *The Boy in the Burgundy Hood*:

***** 'The perfect modern day ghost story with a grisly twist'
***** 'Impossible to put down'
***** 'Creepy and satisfying'
***** 'A compelling and spinetingling read'
***** 'Too scared to sleep… I read it in one day!'
***** 'Turn the screw it does, right up to its terrifyingly dark finale.'

Also in *The Ghosts of Alice* series:

The Girl in the Ivory Dress

Will a strange request help her move on from a haunted past?

After a fire tears through the country house where she works, Alice accepts a desperate invitation from a friend whose guest house is being haunted.

But when Alice arrives at the remote Peacehaven, she senses something much stranger going on. Who is the ghastly spectre roaming the house? Why is he terrifying the guests? And why does Alice keep dreaming about the ghosts of her past, the burning man and girl in the ivory dress?

As she digs deeper, Alice will uncover an insidious evil that might just overwhelm her...

Alice and the Devil

'Yes, I can see ghosts,' she said.

'That's why she told me to come here. Because you can help us. You can help grandad and me. You can help us defeat him.'

'Him?'

'Yes, him. The Devil.'

A boy crosses the moors in a storm to plead for Alice's help, claiming to be sent by a ghost.

Is the boy's grandfather really being terrorised by the Devil himself? Alice can't believe it – but then she's experienced things she'd never imagined could come true. But even with her paranormal experiences, little does she expect the horror she is about to face at the lonely rectory overlooking the moors…

About the Author

Steve Griffin is the author of supernatural thrillers, known for his bestselling *Ghosts of Alice* series. Readers of the latest book, *Alice and the Devil*, call it 'terrifying, thrilling, suspenseful' and a 'compelling and spinetingling read'.

Alongside his ghost stories, he has written an adventure mystery series for young adults, *The Secret of the Tirthas*. The first book, *The City of Light*, was described in *The Guardian* as 'entertaining and exciting.'

Steve loves exploring the Surrey Hills where he lives with his wife and two sons. He likes a good indie gig and is a lifelong lover of spooky movies.

To keep updated on his writing, hit the follow button on Amazon or sign up to his newsletter by emailing stevegriffin.author@outlook.com. You can also check out his website at steve-griffin.com and connect with him on Instagram and Facebook: @stevegriffin.author

.

Printed in Great Britain
by Amazon

28250097R00076